THE GARDENER

THE GARDENER

S.A. BODEEN

FEIWEL AND FRIENDS
NEW YORK

For Tanzie

A FEIWEL AND FRIENDS BOOK
An Imprint of Macmillan

THE GARDENER. Copyright © 2010 by S. A. Bodeen. All rights reserved.
Distributed in Canada by H.B. Fenn and Company, Ltd. Printed in
April 2010 in the United States of America by R. R. Donnelley & Sons Company,
Harrisonburg, Virginia. For information, address
Feiwel and Friends, 175 Fifth Avenue, New York, N.Y. 10010.

Library of Congress Cataloging-in-Publication Data

Bodeen, S. A. (Stephanie A.),
The Gardener / S.A. Bodeen. — 1st ed.
p. cm.
Summary: When high school sophomore Mason finds a beautiful but catatonic
girl in the nursing home where his mother works, the discovery leads him to
revelations about a series of disturbing human experiments that have a
connection to his own life.
ISBN: 978-0-312-37016-9
[1. Experiments—Fiction.   2. Single parent families—Fiction.
3. Fathers—Fiction.   4. Science fiction.]   I. Title.
PZ7.B63515Gar 2010
[Fic]—dc22
2009048802

Book design by Rich Deas

Feiwel and Friends logo designed by Filomena Tuosto

First Edition: 2010

10 9 8 7 6 5 4 3 2 1

www.feiwelandfriends.com

"If you become a mountain climber," said the little bunny,
"I will be a crocus in a hidden garden."
"If you become a crocus in a hidden garden," said his mother,
"I will be a gardener. And I will find you."

—Margaret Wise Brown

PROLOGUE

THE VIDEOTAPE OF MY FATHER WAS NEVER MEANT TO BE SEEN by me, and were it not for a chow mix ripping apart half my face, the man might have remained only a mysterious void. But it was that day when I was five, that day of growls and blood and pain and screams, when I first heard my father's voice.

That morning ten years ago, I waited on the sidewalk for the kindergarten bus. Next door, the Sheffers' dog, Packer, sniffed for a good place on the lawn to poop. I'd known him since he was a pup, and it was my daily ritual to call his name and pet him before the bus arrived. But that day, when my blue untied sneaker touched his lawn, he attacked, charging at me with vicious speed. As I fell backward onto the grass, there was only time for a small squeak to escape my lips: a sound way too tiny for someone to hear, for someone to come running and help. But when my screams started, they were loud enough. Plenty loud enough.

Two screen doors slammed in unison as both Mr. Sheffer and my mother ran outside. A swearing Mr. Sheffer kicked Packer off of me while my mother dropped to her knees, her wide, stricken eyes looking down at me as she said, over and over, "My beautiful boy, my beautiful boy, my beautiful boy—"

Then Mr. Sheffer shouted at her, "For God's sake, help him!"

Snapping out of it, my mother scooped me up and threw me over her shoulder, the front part of me hanging halfway down her back. As she ran with gasping sobs toward the garage, the driveway bounced below me, blood falling from my face, leaving shiny red flowers to bloom on the concrete.

After laying me on the front seat, my head in her lap, she drove to the hospital, screeching around the corners so fast I had to put my hand on the console to keep from falling. In the emergency room, there were whispers mixed in with my mother's frantic pleas and my whimpers and cries, as hands held me down to clean out my wound. The doctor plunged long needles into my face to numb it before he started stitching.

By then, there was no more pain. My eyes wouldn't stay open. I just lay there, eyes shut, feeling an occasional tug on my face as my mother clasped my hand in both of hers.

"Ninety-seven stitches. He's lucky." The doctor's voice was a practiced calm. "No damage to the facial nerves."

He left out the small detail that the damage was too close to those facial nerves to ever risk reconstructive surgery, and one side of my face would look like Frankenstein, but hey, I was *lucky*.

After the emergency room, my mother drove me home.

Her hand shook as she turned up the volume of a *Sesame Street* tune for me, and the inside of the car had a metallic smell. Half of my face was bandaged, including my right eye, which Packer's teeth had narrowly missed. So I peered out my left eye, afraid to move my head, as one of my hands gripped a purple Saf-T-Pop.

My prize for the day.

At home, Mom carried me to the couch and propped me up on a couple of pillows. I still sniffled from crying so much, but thanks to the meds, I was in no pain. Mom kept pacing from room to room, wringing her hands when she wasn't blowing her nose and wiping away tears. After what seemed like a long time, she finally stopped and looked at me. She sighed and shook her head, then went into her room and came back out with a videotape. She slid it into the VCR and sat on the edge of the couch beside me.

With my left eye, I studied her pale, tear-streaked face. Her voice was low and calm. "Mason. I know I've always told you your father was . . . gone. But it's not true. He just can't be your father right now."

Being five, of course I asked when he *could* be my father, but she didn't answer. Just played the tape for me. A recording of a man in a green shirt, shown only as a torso, reading *The Runaway Bunny*. He could have been anyone from anywhere. His voice was not unique, no trace of an accent. Except for the blue butterfly tattooed on his right forearm, nothing about him was distinguishable. Not exactly the father I'd been dreaming about. But I was five and I'd just been scarred for life. And he said the word *son* before he started to read.

So I snuggled against my mom and listened. Really hard.

And when Mr. Sheffer took poor Packer out back, I didn't even hear the gunshot.

O N E

In the last hour of the day, Mr. Hogan's sophomore biology class gathered around to watch the small, green-dotted frilly snail slime its way up my arm. Taller than everyone, I looked down on heads as smells drifted up. To my left, someone had taco breath from lunch. And somewhere to my right was definitely the culprit who'd ripped the little sample of men's cologne out of the school library's latest issue of *Sports Illustrated*.

Hogan rolled his wheelchair closer. Fridays were T-shirt day for the teachers if they paid a buck to the party fund in the office, and his declared Soylent Green Is People! "So this intertidal nudibranch is not just any marine snail."

"Looks like it has a little green wig," said one of the girls.

Our teacher continued. "This snail can photosynthesize. Which means?"

As always, Miranda Collins blurted out the answer before anyone else could. "When a plant uses sunlight to make its own food." Suck-up.

"But this isn't a plant." I couldn't tell who said that, but I was wondering the same thing.

"Aha, we have a genius!" Hogan pointed at the snail.

"That is not a plant. But it eats zooxanthellae, organisms that eat algae. And algae, of course, are plants."

"That makes no sense." Although my eyes were on the snail, I felt heads turn up in my direction and it got quiet. Odd for teenagers, but it probably had to do with the fact that, after the dog incident, I didn't speak in school until fifth grade. I'm not sure if it was due to the trauma, although that's what both the speech pathologist and school psychiatrist told my mom. I think it was more a matter of my not having much to say. But since then, when I did open my mouth in class, it was still considered a bit of a novelty, I guess, because everyone tended to get quiet and listen. "I mean, I eat plants, but I can't photosynthesize. Humans are . . ." I searched for the word we'd just learned that describes organisms that have to get their nutrients from other organisms. "Heterotrophic. We can't feed ourselves."

Hogan nodded. "Exactly. The zooxanthellae evolved so they could retain the cells of the algae, which are responsible for photosynthesis. Evolution, anyone?"

"Changes that take place in a species over time." Miranda again.

"Exactly. And so in the case of the zooxanthellae, you are what you eat. They became autotrophic. Self-feeders. And the nudibranchs have evolved to do the same thing."

"Mr. Hogan?" Miranda Collins waved her hand. "Is this on the quiz?"

He growled at her. "Not everything is on the quiz, but that doesn't mean it's not worth knowing."

6

I moved my arm closer and stared at the snail. "So why is this worth knowing?"

"Well, technically, this proves that an organism can turn autotrophic." He pointed at my arm. "Skin graft those snails all over your body in a sunny climate and eventually you wouldn't have to eat or drink ever again."

A few of the girls let out groans and prolonged *ewwww*s, while some of the boys laughed.

"No, thanks. I like cheeseburgers too much." I gently picked the snail off my arm and set it in the glass tank on Hogan's desk.

"Thanks, Mason." Hogan rolled back behind his desk as we took our seats. "Anyone heard of Giri Bala?"

Most of us either shook our heads or didn't respond at all.

With a remote, he turned on the projector, starting a black-and-white PowerPoint. The first grainy photo showed two old women wrapped in loose, robe-type garments. "This is India, 1936. The woman on the right is Giri Bala, born in 1868."

Jack Meacham sat across the aisle from me. We'd been best friends since kindergarten. Kids had kind of shied away when I stopped speaking, but Jack talked so much he didn't seem to notice I wasn't saying anything. And when we started doing stuff at my house or his, he realized I did have things to say. But in school, he spoke for both of us until fifth grade, when I finally started talking again. I'd gradually outgrown him, and everyone else, by about eighty pounds and six inches. Two pairs of his Levi's sewn together might just encase one of my thighs. He raised his hand. "Who was she?"

Hogan grinned. "You mean who *is* she?"

Jack glanced at me, and then lines appeared between his eyebrows. "If she was born in 1868, she'd be, like . . ."

I could see him doing the math in his head. Although Jack had high aspirations to become a doctor, he struggled in school. Not for lack of trying. He was really smart but just had some kind of mental block on test days. He shook his head slightly. "Well, she'd be way over one hundred. Impossible."

"Maybe not." Hogan clasped his hands together. "At the time this photo was taken, Giri Bala had not eaten for fifty-six years."

The class erupted with sounds of disbelief. I even let loose with a "No way."

Holding up his hand for silence, Hogan explained. "She supposedly used a yoga technique that allowed her to get her energy from the sun. The leader of her province actually locked her in a room for several days with no food or water, and she was perfectly fine. And some people say she's still alive."

The next picture came up, a view of Moscow and the Kremlin. "There's a group of people living in Moscow who claim to be autotrophs. They started out as vegans, gradually stopped eating all food, and now claim they neither eat nor drink."

I shook my head as someone called out, "That's crazy."

"Maybe so." Hogan nodded. "But one scientist claims he can take a human, put him in a tropical climate, and turn his body into a living solar cell within two years."

8

Jack raised his hand. Even in classes like Hogan's, where we were allowed to just speak up if we had something productive to say, Jack still raised his hand every time he had something to say. "But why would you want to do that? Save your lunch money or something?"

Hogan smiled. "Think about it, Jack. Imagine having an army you don't have to feed or water."

The bell rang. "Don't forget, quiz on Monday!" A few groans erupted, and before I could get up, Hogan called my name. "See me after class."

I asked Jack if he could give me a ride home.

He nodded and said, "Meet you in the parking lot."

Everyone filed out and I went up to the front. Hogan held up a sheet I recognized, the application form for the TroDyn summer science program. He shook it at me. "You know the deadline is coming up for this?"

TroDyn Industries was a huge scientific complex on a hundred acres looking over Melby Falls. Mainly working on environmental sustainability projects, the company supported the town. Although they didn't employ many townspeople at their lab facilities, TroDyn owned most of the businesses, including the nursing home where my mom worked, and they paid for a lot of equipment and supplies at the school. I'd read about the summer program, and Hogan had told us about it several times. "My mom would never go for it. She's not a TroDyn fan." It might just be a case of not liking the company responsible for your sucky job, but she had no lack of bad things to say about them.

Hogan tapped the paper with a finger. "If you do the

summer program, you'll have a good shot at the TroDyn scholarship." His eyes met mine, but not in a forced way. I mean, some people stare at my scar. I don't mind, at least it's honest, and when they've seen enough, they meet my eyes. But the ones who lock eyes with me, those are the dishonest ones. You can almost hear them chanting to themselves *Don't look at his scar, don't look at his scar.* Hogan's eyes met mine the way his eyes met anyone else's.

I shrugged. "I'm not really sure about college."

"Mason, come on." Hogan waved the paper. "You're one of the smartest kids I've ever had in class."

"Miranda Collins is smarter."

Hogan rolled his eyes. "I suspect Miranda Collins gets A's because she spends three hours a night memorizing textbooks. Probably polishes a lot of apples while she's at it. A potato could do that and get A's. You actually understand this stuff. You get it. You need to go to college and learn more."

I didn't say anything.

"They'll cover all your college expenses through grad school. They would pay for Stanford."

I rolled my eyes. "Like I'd get into Stanford."

"I've seen your standardized test scores. On the SAT, you'll smoke kids like Miranda Collins. You'll get in." He flipped the paper onto the desk, where it settled next to the stapler. "All they ask in return is that you commit to working five years in their labs."

Other than getting my mom on board, I didn't see the problem with that. I looked around at his biology room, my favorite place in the school. The shelves were lined with not only glossy books but pristine specimens in glass jars of whatever the liquid was that replaced formaldehyde. I'd always been drawn to the framed glass cases that housed expensive collections of bugs and butterflies and spiders. A bank of desktop computers lined one wall, and I knew them to be loaded with more biological research software than most college libraries held, courtesy of TroDyn.

I'd be lying to say I didn't want to go to college. I'd also be lying to say I didn't really *really* like biology. Going to Stanford to study biology, on a full ride no less, would be a dream come true. But it wasn't easy for me to put my dreams out for everyone to see. I preferred to keep them to myself so only I was disappointed when they didn't happen. That way, I didn't have to have people telling me how sorry they were for me. I'd had enough of that to last my entire life.

Trying to shift the focus, I asked, "Do they bribe you to talk kids into this?"

He held up his hands in a gesture of surrender. "You're right. I mean, you can probably get a scholarship another way. Not to Stanford, but you're the best offensive tackle Melby Falls has seen in a while."

I saw his point. "Yeah, that just might pay for my books at a junior college." I picked up the application, pretending to read as if I'd never seen it before, when actually there was one half filled out in my locker, plus three extras at home, hidden in my copy of last year's yearbook.

He leaned back. "Think about it."

"Okay." I smiled.

He shrugged. "Come on, Al Gore gave them that award last year for making progress with global warming research. They do a lot of good things up there. You could save the world someday."

"Yeah, right." I shoved the application into my biology book.

"Due Monday!" he called after me.

Out in the hall at my locker, I hooked my backpack on my arm and hoisted it over my shoulder. My locker clicked shut just as I heard one in the junior high hallway bang a couple of times. And then I heard a muffled cry.

In two steps, I was around the corner. Two smaller boys were up against the lockers as a bigger boy stood in front of them, a hand over one boy's mouth.

"Hey."

They all turned and looked at me. The bigger one dropped his hand and stepped back. I'd seen him around, was named Wendell or Walker or something like that.

"Problem here?"

The two against the lockers shook their heads while the other one crossed his arms. "Oh, hey, Mason. No, no problem."

Taking a few steps closer, I said, "To me, it looks like there's a problem."

The bigger kid's eyes darted around and he began backing away from me.

I told the smaller boys, "Go home."

They both nodded and ran as I walked toward the other kid and backed him into the wall. There were still a few feet between us, but he was breathing harder and his eyes were wide. And why not? Most kids who didn't know me very well kept their distance. I was big, and my scar made my face look scary. But I used it to my advantage on bullies like him.

"You need to leave those kids alone."

He nodded.

"Seriously. I catch you picking on anyone else . . ." For effect, I made a fist and covered it with my other hand. "Got it?"

He didn't say anything, just ran off down the hall.

I smiled as I dropped my hands. Off the football field, I would never think of hurting anyone, but most people probably didn't know that. They just saw a big, Halloween-masked hulk of a guy. But what a rush, to save people. The first time was when I was in fifth grade. After school, I usually headed to the Bottoms, a forest walking trail. One day I heard someone calling for help. Going off the trail a ways, I found a couple of second-grade girls. They'd been messing around, playing by a pile of logs, and one girl had gotten her foot caught. So I managed to roll the log off and carried the girl all the way back to the school. Her grandma was one of the teachers, and I got my picture in the paper. That part was kind of weird. I don't like my picture getting taken, and I made sure to turn my head so only my good side showed. The coolest part for me was just seeing the relief on the face of the grandma when she hugged the kids, especially when things could have turned out differently. Being responsible for the happy ending made me happy.

After that, I saved people every chance I got.

Outside, there was a light drizzle, and I jogged to where Jack waited for me in his red truck, Deep Purple turned up so high that I'd heard it the second I'd stepped outside. "Thanks for waiting." Jack and I shared a lot of the same tastes, including the one for old rock music.

I reached over and turned the volume up even more.

Although he got the Ford for his birthday a couple of months before, the inside still smelled new. His dad owned a chain of plumbing supply stores in the Pacific Northwest; Jack was rich and could pay for any college he got into. But with his grades, the problem was getting in. So he worried about things like SAT scores while I worried about my bank account.

I asked, "What time are we leaving?"

Jack's family owned a cabin up in Glenwood, at the foot of Mount Adams, and we planned to head up there for the weekend to go ATV'ing. Not only did they own a batch of the finest new Arctic Cats, they also had acres and acres of trails to ride around on. Plus, it was the first weekend we'd be going since Jack got his license, our first weekend out of town on our own.

But as he pulled out of the parking lot, he said, "We'll have to wait and go tomorrow. I just got called in to work."

"So don't go." I drew circles in the fog on my window. "It's not like you need the money."

"Turn down an extra shift at the Haven of Peace?" If he did get into college, Jack planned to go premed. Can't say he didn't aim high. So when he turned sixteen, he took a job as an orderly at the same nursing home where my mom worked. He turned into my driveway and let the Ford idle. "Besides, I'm saving up to take Miranda Collins to prom." He also got a hefty allowance, so I doubt he would have to save up for long.

I made a face. "She's such a brown-noser. You haven't said one word to her since she tore up your valentine in sixth grade."

He grinned. "I admire her . . . um . . . intelligence from afar."

"Intelligence my ass."

Jack laughed. "And destiny is on my side."

"You've been saying that since sixth grade. Destiny hasn't helped you get a girl yet, dude."

He reached over and punched me. "With all this rain, we probably can't do most of the trails anyway."

The only problem with the area around Jack's cabin was that the trails were steep and did get treacherous in downpours like we'd been having. I told him, "I still wanna get out of town. We can always just play Halo."

When he reached my driveway, I said, "Call me if you get off early." I got out and slammed the door.

"Watch it!"

I waved my hand without looking back.

Inside, the house was quiet. "Mom? You home?" I waited for a response, but there was none, so I made a couple of bologna sandwiches and sat down at the table, pulling my biology book and the slightly wrinkled TroDyn application out of my backpack. Mom wouldn't be as supportive as Hogan.

I'd decided my plan was to forge her signature and tell her I got a job for the summer. I knew her signature was always handy on the fridge in the form of that month's rent check, pinned in place by a strawberry-shaped magnet. But the check wasn't there.

I knelt and looked around the floor first, then up at the calendar. The twenty-eighth. Wow, she must have paid rent early for once.

After finishing my second sandwich, I wondered if her signature was on something else. Canceled checks maybe. So I headed into her room, where she kept the little brown filing cabinet, and I yanked the handle. Locked, as always. I'd seen the drawers open before, like when I needed my birth certificate or something else official. But then Mom always locked it back up.

The phone by Mom's bed startled me. I grabbed it on the beginning of the second ring.

"Honey?"

"Mom?"

"Can you come get me? I'm at the Brass Rail." Her words slurred.

My hand clenched the phone and my shoulders slumped. Although I already knew the answer, I asked, "What are you doing?"

"I just stopped by for a quick shot, I swear."

Sounded more like several quick shots to me. I sighed. "Okay, I'm coming." Snatching the car keys off her night-stand, I hurried outside.

Never mind that I wouldn't get my license for another

four months, when I turned sixteen, I'd been driving my mother around town for the last year. Before that, when she got in one of her moods, she did a lot of walking home from bars. It didn't happen that often, my driving. But it happened more than it should, I suppose. Especially recently, when she seemed to be having way more of her moods than usual.

I backed the Jeep out of the driveway and headed downtown, meaning via the one street in town that went straight through. Melby Falls was about ten miles off I-5, and I couldn't think of many reasons for anyone ever to visit. We did have our own TroDyn-funded municipal police force, one member of which waved to me as I turned onto Main Street. As long as you didn't break laws flamboyantly, they left you alone. Handy for underage drivers like myself.

I pulled into the handicapped space by the front door of the Brass Rail, just as the front door was flung open and my mother came out, escorted by a burly man in a red polo. He'd bounced Mom before. I didn't know his name, but I'm pretty sure something on the order of Bubba would fit.

Mom wore jeans and a white sweater, which had some kind of reddish stain all down the front. Her dark hair blew in her face as she tried to smile at me. "Mason."

Bubba wrenched open the Jeep's door and practically shoved her up into the seat.

Despite being pissed at my mom for getting drunk, I wasn't going to let someone hurt her. I knew it must have been hard for her, raising me on her own, working at a job she didn't like. Having a few too many drinks once in a while didn't make her a bad mother. "Hey, take it easy." Resisting the urge to step out of the car and show Bubba I wasn't afraid to take him, I gripped Mom's arm and helped her in.

Bubba's gaze fixed on my scar before going back up to meet my eyes. His voice was low and firm. "Take her home, sober her up. And keep her out of here. Better for her if she keeps her opinions to herself."

Inwardly, I groaned. Did it always have to be the same story? It was one thing for Mom to bash TroDyn at home, completely something else to trash them in public while intoxicated. As I leaned over her to fasten her seat belt, her hand on my arm stopped me and I looked into her teary eyes. Among other things, I wanted to chew her out for drinking again. Instead, I asked, "You okay?"

She nodded. Her eyes wandered to my scar and she reached up with her fingertips, tracing it lightly all the way to my jaw.

After so long, I'd gotten used to my face. Things might have been better if they could have just sewed it straight up. But a few pieces were missing here and there, making the scar look somewhat like a quilt in places where the doctor had pulled the torn skin together. One end of the scar started at my right eye's outside corner, making my eye look a little like it sagged. That line of the scar met another at the top of my right cheek, and two parts branched out from there, one ending near my mouth, the other trailing off the side of my chin.

Jack said it made me look tough, like some of those guys

in the movies. That didn't matter to me, looking tough. It might've been nice on the football field except my helmet covered it up anyway. And really, at almost six feet three and two hundred thirty pounds, I didn't exactly come across as weak. Plus, there was no need to play a tough guy. If things worked out, if I actually did get into college, I planned to spend most of my adult life in a lab somewhere, hence the appeal of TroDyn, where appearances had no bearing on daily lives.

My classmates had been my classmates since I was in kindergarten. I showed up that week after the attack with a bandage, then the bandage came off, my scar was revealed, and for a few weeks it was big news. Then, as my silence grew, my celebrity and the scar began to fade. I was just Mason, my scar a part of me. And as I grew bigger than everyone in school, most saw me simply as this hulking quiet guy.

Maybe that was one reason for me to stay in Melby Falls after college, if I managed to go. Me, and my scar, were familiar. Out in the world I might just be the freak with the scar on his face. I liked being more than the sum of my parts. I also liked not having to deal with that shocked look people got upon seeing my face for the first time.

Mom set her whole hand on the right side of my face. "You're still my beautiful boy. I don't know what I'd do without you."

"For starters, you'd need to call a cab." I snapped her seat belt and settled back.

She leaned her head on the window. "Something is

wrong. Ever since the money stopped coming. I just feel it."

"What?"

Mom had a funny look on her face, like she was surprised I'd heard her. But instead of answering me, she shook her head and didn't say another word the entire ride.

Back home, I made Mom a pot of strong coffee. Caffeine would just make her a wide-awake drunk, rather than truly sober her, but it always helped. With a wince, I remembered my TroDyn application just as she plopped down at the table and picked up the sheaf of papers.

T W O

My mother wouldn't have been able to make out the small print in her condition, but the large TroDyn insignia on top had to be unmistakable even to someone with blurred vision.

Slapping the papers down with her hand, she glared at me. "What are you thinking?"

I sat down opposite her. "It's the summer program. It's my best chance to get a scholarship."

"No." She slurped some coffee and repeated the word several times until I finally asked her to stop.

Trying to keep my voice soft and steady, I said, "Mom, we've got to be practical here. I need a college education, and you can't afford it."

She pushed the papers away from her. "There's a fund." She was hard to understand.

"A what?"

"A fund. A college fund. For you."

I rolled my eyes and stifled a laugh. "Yeah, okay, Mom. You barely make enough money to keep the electricity on every month. You sure don't make enough to have a college fund for me."

She was quiet for a moment. "You're right." Her eyes met mine. "It's not *my* money."

"Whose is it, then?"

For a moment, she didn't answer, like she was considering not saying anything else.

"Mom?"

She sighed. "Your father. Your father started the fund."

I gripped the sides of the chair. "What?" He can't be my father but he can start a college fund for me? I didn't believe her. This was just a convenient excuse to get me to not go to TroDyn. And then I wouldn't go to college, and then . . .

I picked up the application.

She ripped it out of my hand. "You're not going anywhere near that place."

As we glared at each other, the phone rang several times until I finally let out a huge sigh and got up to answer it. Mom's work. I covered the mouthpiece. "It's the Haven. They want to confirm you're working at eight. You're not, are you?"

Her forehead wrinkled. "What day is it?"

I blew out a deep breath. "Are you serious? It's Friday."

"But I don't work on—" She dropped her head in her hands and groaned. "I forgot! I switched with Burt."

Although our little Cape Cod house had pretty low rent, we would be in trouble if she lost her job. All those pesky little things that required money, like lights and water and, oh yeah, food. We'd been lucky so far; the Haven of Peace gave her overtime, health insurance, and retirement. The hours sucked, four nights a week, but then she had three days off. And she managed to save her drinking for those days, which worked fine unless she forgot her schedule.

"Mom?"

She headed for her room. "Tell them I'll be there."

As I threw some leftover curried chicken in the oven for dinner, the shower started, signifying Mom was on her way back to the land of the sober. I set the timer on the oven. I'd been the only kid in the cooking class at the library, but it came in handy on the nights when Mom was in no condition to cook. I mean, 80 percent of the time, she was a fully functioning mom, cleaning the house, cooking, keeping me in line. But the rest of the time, I had to step up.

In my room, I plopped down on the weight bench in front of my TV and shoved in the DVD of my father. I'd watched the videotape so many times since the day of my accident that it had nearly worn out, so I had it transferred to a DVD. Of which I burned twenty copies. Just in case. Nineteen of them were in a box under my bed. One was in my DVD player.

When I was small, I watched it a lot, nearly every day, but as I got older, the urge grew less frequent. Still, it became a bit of a security blanket I couldn't give up. And when Mom and I fought, usually when she'd been drinking, it was a comfort to flick it on and see what I'd seen a thousand times before. Because there was something about watching it, something that happened to me. The video sucked me in, magically put me in a sort of trance, giving me a reprieve from my life.

Like always, I froze as the video flickered on.

My father, or rather his green-shirted torso, sat in a chair in front of a yellow wall. *The Runaway Bunny* was in his hands, which were a darker skin tone than mine. The first time I noticed the color of his skin, things clicked into place. I'd always wondered how I could've gotten my dark skin from my paler-than-pale mom. Watching the video was like understanding where I fit, somewhere between the woman who cared for me and this man, this man I'd never met. I studied the footage every time I watched it, always with this little bit of hope that I'd discover something else about him.

Or about myself.

But it was the same every time, no more buried treasure to be found. His voice is deep and he reads clearly and well. The text is all on pages with black-and-white illustrations, divided by a full page in color with no words. At one part of the story, my favorite part, the one where the bunny wants to go be a crocus in a hidden garden, he turns the book to himself and pauses, turning the page before showing the camera again. And, for just a second, his right sleeve slips up, revealing a tattoo on his forearm. A blue butterfly.

"Mason!"

I tore myself away, clicked the remote to PAUSE, and went into the master bedroom. The bathroom door was shut. I knocked. "Mom?"

She opened the door, standing there with a blue towel wrapped around her, hands streaked with blood.

Grabbing a towel to staunch the flow coming from her

shin, I dropped to my knees in front of her. I shook my head and muttered, "You shouldn't shave your legs when you're drunk."

Her hand rested on top of my head. "I can't go to work like this."

"Mom, you have to. You used up all your sick days for the month."

"I'm in no condition to work." Her voice was whiny.

I just wanted to tell her to shut up. But that wouldn't help, so I made certain my voice was quiet. "That's all we need—for you to get fired."

She sounded even more agitated. "Which they will do if they see I'm not sober."

There was only one solution I could think of, and it was a terrible idea. "I can go with you, help you do your work."

She sank down on the bed. "You can't do that."

There never had been any reason for me to go to the Haven of Peace, and I struggled to think of ways to make the idea sound less idiotic. None came to mind. I said, "Mom, come on. I'll just stay a while until you're completely fine, and then I'll sneak out and go home." I'd nearly convinced myself it was a good idea.

"No." Her hand patted my head. "I'll be fine. Night shift is easy."

I sat down on the bed and put an arm around her. "Let me drive you at least?"

"Okay." She leaned into me for just a moment before heading back into the bathroom.

Enabling her like that wasn't good, I knew, but she was

my mom. What else could I do? I tossed the bloodstained towel into the laundry room sink and then filled it with cold water to soak. Back in the kitchen, I cleaned off the table, setting Mom's purse on the edge of the counter, where I promptly knocked it off with my elbow when I swung back around.

Her crap was all over the floor, and I started shoveling it back in, when I saw her Curves key chain with a small key on it. Like the kind of key that might fit the filing cabinet in her bedroom. I glanced toward the bedroom once, then slipped the key off and put it in my back pocket.

Black Sabbath blared from the front pocket of my jeans. I flipped my silver phone open. Jack said, "Hey, we can go tonight after all. I get off at nine."

I glanced at the clock and did the math. I would still have time to drop Mom off and then come back to the house to finish the TroDyn application, forged signature and all. And maybe go on a little treasure hunt. "Cool."

Right.

To save time, I packed a backpack to take to Jack's cabin, throwing in the DVD. I always took a copy when I went out of town, the way other people might stick a family photo in their wallet. Maybe it was weird, but I just felt better knowing it was there, in case I wanted, or needed, to watch it. Jack had known about the tape since we were in grade school and never gave me any grief. He knew what it meant to me.

After dropping Mom off at Haven of Peace, I drove home and went right into her room to try the filing cabinet. The key turned easily. My hand rested on the handle, but I didn't pull. It was an invasion of my mom's privacy. But I couldn't help wondering if there might be something interesting in the file cabinet. Maybe something from my father?

Like a college fund? I couldn't help but roll my eyes.

Still, I started to look. One folder held tax files. I flipped through them. The signature line was blank, the TurboTax electronic signature jotted down beside it instead.

My heart was beating harder. "This is crazy," I muttered. Did I really expect to find some secret about her past? Of course, didn't every kid wish that? Instead of being stuck with the parent we have, didn't we all want to discover they were way cooler than reality?

I sighed as I set the tax files down. The only secret past my mom had was that she had a kid with some guy who was no longer in the picture. Not exactly a rare thing.

My hand got caught when I reached for more files. As I yanked it out, something fell off the bottom of the top drawer.

A manila envelope lined with crackling, yellowed Scotch tape.

With a quick glance at the doorway, even though I knew Mom was at work, I stared at the envelope she'd hidden. I'd be lying if I said I believed the video of my father was the only thing she'd ever kept from me. I didn't suspect big secrets, but I sensed there could be smaller things that might affect me. Part of me figured the envelope was the only thing she'd ever kept from me. And that part of me decided to take the envelope into the kitchen and open it.

A small laminated card fell out first, a miniature diploma. From Duke University. Upon closer inspection, I saw my mom's name and her degree. My mouth nearly dropped. My mom had a master's? I pulled something else out, a white envelope with the return address of a financial firm. Inside, I found a notice dated six months ago, stating that automatic deposits had been suspended. That was about the time Mom started drinking more.

I set that aside and reached inside the manila envelope again, pulling out another small card. That one had a picture of my mom, and the insignia above it was one I knew well. It was on my application.

My jaw dropped.

It was an ID card for TroDyn. Not like the ID card she had for the Haven, which didn't mention the name Tro-Dyn. My mom had worked for the labs?

I lifted my backpack off the kitchen table, then ran out to the Jeep and tried not to speed as I headed for Haven of Peace. It had to be a mistake. Maybe it was an old name tag from the Haven, maybe they used to have the TroDyn logo on them. At a stop sign, I turned on the dome light and studied the ID. No mention of the Haven. And in the picture, my mother wore a white lab coat. Definitely not an ID from a nursing home.

I'd wanted a secret past. Maybe I'd really found one.

At the final stop sign before the nursing home, I called Jack. "Can you get me into the Haven?"

"I thought I was coming to get you at nine?"

I gripped the steering wheel with my free hand, squeezing

out my frustration. "Yeah, you were. But I've gotta get in to see my mom."

"Hmmm." I heard him moving around. "Okay. Do you have your mom's key card to get in the parking lot?"

I flipped down the visor, and a card fell into my lap. "Yup."

"Okay, use that to get into the parking lot and drive to the far end."

Keeping the phone at my ear, I followed his instructions. The card machine beeped as a red light on the security camera overhead blinked. After parking, I turned off the car. "Now what?"

"See the hedge along the wall?" Jack was breathing hard.

"Yeah. What are you doing?"

"Helping Mrs. O'Connell get into bed." His voice became a whisper. "And she's no small girl."

A ten-foot-tall concrete wall surrounded the parking lot on all sides, with a continuous hedge broken in one spot for a sidewalk. "Do I follow that sidewalk?"

"Yeah, it leads to a side door. Meet you there in two minutes."

Trying not to look suspicious, I slung my backpack over my shoulder and kept my strides normal as I headed for the door. Jack's two minutes stretched into eight, but finally he met me there with a huge, white orderly jumpsuit, which I quickly threw on over my clothes. He handed me a name badge.

I glanced at the name. "Steve?"

Jack grinned. "Steve had the night off, until now." He pointed me up the stairs. "Sixth floor."

I waited for him to lead the way, but he started to turn.

I asked, "You're not coming?"

"I'm only allowed on the first floor," said Jack. He glanced at his watch. "It's almost eight thirty, so I'll meet you in the parking lot in about thirty minutes. Just wait at that far end. Oh, and, Mace?"

"Yeah?"

He pointed at my name tag. "Steve isn't allowed on other floors either. So don't get caught."

THREE

THE DOOR TO THE STAIRS CREAKED OPEN WHEN I PULLED, then closed with a *whoosh* behind me as I started climbing. After six flights I stepped into a large carpeted room painted green.

Mom was there at the counter in the middle, and her eyes widened when she saw me. "You can't be here. Where did you get that uniform?"

I walked right over and shoved a finger toward her. "You are such a hypocrite."

Her mouth opened, like she was going to say something, then it popped shut again.

My words came out in a loud rush. "I know you worked for TroDyn. I found your ID, your diploma from Duke. A master's degree, Mom? What else haven't you told me?"

Her eyes narrowed. "You broke into my files?"

"Yes, I did." I held up my hands. "I'm sorry. But is it worse than you lying to me all this time?"

"I didn't lie." Her shoulders sagged. "I just omitted a few things."

"Keeping things from me is just as bad as lying."

She shook her head, a small smile on her face. "Oh no, it isn't."

31

Like every time she got drunk or made some stupid decision, I remembered she was my mother, and the only family I had. The realization always made me soften. No matter how I tried to stay firm, that made it hard for me to stay angry at her. "So what else, Mom? What else don't I know?"

Lowering her voice, she leaned over the counter toward me. "Mason, this is not the right time or place for this conversation."

I looked around the room. There were a few patients sitting in front of a big-screen television set, so I lowered my voice a bit. "You're right." I crossed my arms. "The right time would have been years ago. I'm not leaving here until you tell me why I just found a TroDyn badge in your room."

Letting out a big sigh, she took a swig of coffee from a blue cup on the counter, then set it down. "You know the first part. I grew up in a small town in the Midwest, not much money, and I wanted to go to college. Halfway through my undergrad in biology, a TroDyn rep came on campus and offered me a deal. They'd pay for my master's degree if I worked for them afterward."

Where was the mystery in that? I didn't get it. "And what was so bad?"

With a finger, she traced through the wet ring the coffee cup left on the counter, smearing the moisture. "It wasn't what I expected. A lot of pressure and deadlines. I just wasn't cut out for the research, I guess."

I rolled my eyes. "But you're cut out for the nursing home."

She looked at me, then away.

A master's degree, a promising career, and she threw it away. "But why did you stay here? Why didn't you leave?"

She shrugged. "I had you, but I didn't have a lot of resources. It was easy to stay. Harder to start over somewhere."

I slammed a fist on the counter. "That's it? That's all?" Where did my father figure into it? Was he the reason she had no money? Why she had to start over? There had to be more. "You throw away your life and that's it? End of story?"

"I had a baby to think about!" She pounded her fist down next to mine and I jumped. "So yes! End of story!" She jabbed a finger in the air toward me. "I have my issues, I admit that. But you are my son and I have always done what was needed to put a roof over your head. And you will go to college. I told you there's a—" She stopped.

I glanced over toward the patients, but they seemed to be ignoring us. Besides, I didn't really care who heard.

I groaned. Did she still think this was about the summer program? That I was selfish? God, I was thinking about her, about how our lives would be so different if she were pulling in a salary at TroDyn. I wanted to ask her about the statement I found, but just then a timer went off.

"We can finish this later." Mom sighed. "I need to take their vitals."

While she gathered what she needed, I looked around at

floor six, which seemed to be just the one big room, as far as I could tell. Nearly one entire wall was a fish tank, and looking closer, I saw saltwater species. Not cheap by any means. A big-screen television was mounted on the opposite wall, surrounded by several couches, on one of which sat four people. Reruns of *Gilligan's Island* played, but they just sat there, facing the television, shoulder to shoulder, not moving or laughing.

I moved around to see their faces.

My jaw dropped as I saw they were young, all of them. I thought the Haven had only old people. But the two boys and two girls sitting there were my age or even younger, and dressed alike in long-sleeved white T-shirts and red sweatpants with white stripes. I needn't have worried about the argument bothering them. They weren't reacting to the television at all. In fact, they seemed catatonic.

I waved my hand in front of the boy nearest to me and he didn't even flinch. Then my eyes rested on the girl next to him and I froze. Her hair was platinum blond, cut short, so short as to seem almost a mistake. Huge brown eyes filled her face and were such a contrast to the lightness of her hair that she appeared almost unreal, like she was simply someone's portrait. Her skin nearly glowed. I started to feel lightheaded and realized I'd been holding my breath. I let it out in a rush as I continued to stare at the most beautiful girl I had ever seen. Some of my friends were girls, but other than a forced pairing with Lucy Pierson when we got voted freshman reps for the homecoming court, I hadn't dated much. Meaning not at all.

As I'd done with the boy, I waved a hand in front of her face. Nothing. I squatted before her, my eyes starting at the top of her head and running down the length of her. Despite just sitting there, doing nothing, she looked really in shape. Actually, really hot, as Jack would say. On her feet were white flip-flops, and her toenails were painted pink.

"I did that."

Mom's voice startled me and I stood up. "What?"

Mom pointed. "Her toes. I painted them."

I asked, "Who are they? What's wrong with them?"

Mom held up a clipboard and a blood pressure cuff. "Brain injuries."

I looked back at them. "Do they ever do anything?"

Mom shook her head. "This is all I've ever seen them do."

It was so strange. Four healthy-looking teenagers just sitting there.

Mom slipped the cuff onto one of the boys. "Traumatic brain injuries can wreak havoc. Especially on the young." She looked pointedly at my scar. "Sometimes the visible scars are easier to deal with."

My hand went briefly to my face before I sat down on a nearby chair. "Why aren't their parents taking care of them?"

With one hand, she pumped the rubber bulb. *Swsssh, swssh, swssh.* "They require more care than you'd expect. They're also part of a clinical trial."

Brain-dead teenage guinea pigs. And I thought *my* life sucked.

Mom said, "Get that clipboard and write down what I tell you."

I wrote what she dictated as she continued to check the blood pressure of each one. I asked, "How often do you have to do that?"

She glanced at the clock. "Every half hour."

Her attitude seemed so blasé, those kids didn't seem to faze her. And then I realized why. They were her routine. "Why didn't you ever tell me this is who you take care of?"

Mom put a hand on her hip. "Why didn't you ever ask me who I take care of?"

She had me there. But it was a nursing home. Weren't nursing homes for old people? "I just assumed . . ."

She smiled. "The geezers are on the lower floors."

I grinned.

The phone rang and she went to answer it. Then she turned back to me. "Sweetie, I have to go up to floor seven for a bit."

"Who's on that floor?"

"Just offices, no patients."

I only had about twenty minutes before I met Jack. "Can you come back so we can talk about this?"

Mom sighed. "Mason, please. I really want you to get rid of that uniform and go home. Can we just discuss this tomorrow?"

Now that I was actually getting somewhere, and finding out what she'd been hiding from me, I really didn't want to put it off. "I'm meeting Jack at nine. We're still going to the cabin. Oh." I pulled the keys to the Jeep out of my pocket and gave them to her. "It's in the back of the parking lot."

She tossed them once and caught them in her hand. "Wait for me, I'll try to get back before you go."

I glanced at the four on the couch. "What about them?"

Mom shrugged. "They're not going anywhere." She left.

As I picked up my backpack, the case with the DVD of my father started to fall out. I grabbed for it but missed as the back of my hand sent the thing flying. The case hit the side of the counter with a clunk and broke open. The DVD rolled out, coming to a stop underneath the couch.

I went over to the couch and snapped my fingers in front of one of the boys, then waved my entire hand. "Hello?"

He stared straight ahead at the television.

"Hey, ugly!"

His eyes didn't waver.

I faked a punch at his face.

Nothing.

On my hands and knees, I reached under the couch for the DVD and started to put it back in the case. My hands were shaking, as my mind swam with the events of the day. Dealing with Bubba at the bar, my fight with Mom, finding the TroDyn ID. And then, being in a room with catatonic teenagers. It was too much. No wonder my hands were shaking. I needed something to draw me back. Like my father's voice.

I checked the time, then slipped the DVD into the player. I grabbed the remote and sat on the floor with my back leaning against the couch nearest the blond girl. I could smell whatever soap she'd last used. Or had been used on her.

Immediately, I felt myself relax as the DVD started to play, and hoped I would have time to watch the whole thing before my mom got back. My father got to my favorite part. *"I will be a crocus in a hidden garden."*

A soft but hoarse voice startled me. "Where am I?"

I turned.

The beautiful girl's brown eyes, unbelievably vibrant, unmistakably awake, locked with mine.

I couldn't speak.

"If you become a crocus in a hidden garden," said his mother, "I will be a gardener. And I will find you."

My father was still reading. I hit the PAUSE button. "Crap."

The girl's eyes dulled.

"Hello?" I snapped my fingers in front of her face. Nothing.

Then I turned the DVD back on and watched her. Still nothing. My father finished and she was as catatonic as ever. I restarted the DVD and hit PLAY.

"If you become a mountain climber," said the little bunny, "I will be a crocus in a hidden garden."

Again, the girl spoke. "Where am I?"

This time I got out a few words. "Haven of Peace."

"If you become a crocus in a hidden garden," said his mother, "I will be a gardener. And I will find you."

Again, she was gone.

I swore, then went back to the same part.

"If you become a mountain climber," said the little bunny, "I will be a crocus in a hidden garden."

Her voice was becoming familiar and less hoarse. "Where am I?"

This time, I hit PAUSE, then knelt in front of her. "Haven of Peace." I held my breath. *Please please please stay awake, beautiful girl.*

Her brow furrowed. How strange to see an expression on her previously blank face. The confusion made her look even lovelier. Her eyes stayed on mine, then tracked down the length of my scar and back up. With one hand, she touched the left side of my face. No one but my mother or doctors had ever touched my face, and her touch was warm and soft, sending tingles down that whole side of my body. "This side is perfect." Then, with a fingertip, she started at the top of my scar and traced around all the edges. "This side is marked."

I felt myself getting warm, so I leaned back and put a hand on the floor, just to make a little more space between us.

She looked around the room, then back to me. "Who are you?"

"Mason. I . . . my mom works here."

Then she tilted her head. "Who am I?"

"I don't know." I was confused. "You were in an accident and . . ." I trailed off because I didn't really know what had happened to her. I just assumed it had been an accident and realized I shouldn't be telling her anything.

She looked at the others and started to say something.

"If you become a crocus in a hidden garden," said his mother, "I will be a gardener. And I will find you."

39

Her eyes went blank again.

"No!" The PAUSE feature must have had a timer to automatically start up. I restarted, played the part that woke her up, then hit the OFF button and pulled out the DVD.

"What happened?"

I held up the DVD. "I played this and it woke you up. But it also put you back under. So I just played the wake-up part again. . . ." *Idiot. Shut up.*

She put both hands to her face and rubbed, then started to look herself over, flex muscles and things. And that's when the sleeve of her white shirt slipped up and I saw a tattoo. A tattoo on her right forearm. A tattoo of a blue butterfly. Maybe it was just the lighting of the room, but I could have sworn it was the same as the one on my father's arm.

I didn't even have time to think about it. When she saw the tattoo, she started repeating the same phrase, gradually getting louder: "Don't let the gardener find me, don't let the gardener find me, don't let the gardener find me. . . ."

I didn't know what to do, so I just told the girl it would be okay. It didn't seem to help. She got quieter, but she still kept saying it over and over.

"Don't let the gardener find me."

Was she somehow upset over that line from *The Runaway Bunny?* Whatever the reason, she was really creeping me out.

The girl stopped talking suddenly and looked at me. "I need to leave."

I tried to smile a bit, and made sure my voice was calm and reassuring. "My mom will be back in a minute and—"

"The gardener will find me!" Her eyes were misting over as she looked at me. "Please, help me." The girl put a hand on each side of her head and started to moan.

My mom came back in then and took one look at the girl. "What did you do? How did she wake up?" Her hand flew to her chest.

I kind of expected a different reaction as Mom grabbed the girl's arm and started to take her pulse.

"This is good, right?" I asked her. "You can call her parents, tell them she's awake."

Mom's head moved from side to side, almost slow motion as she continued to stare at the girl. "She's not supposed to wake up." Her voice lowered to a whisper. "They aren't ever supposed to wake up."

What kind of freak show was this? Mom was acting so weird.

"I don't understand how this could have happened." Mom's hands shook as she noticed me watching her. "I have to tell someone, so they can take her." She wasn't making sense.

I asked, "You mean call her parents, right? So they can take her home?"

Mom finally snapped out of it and dropped the girl's arm as she looked at me. "No, I don't mean her parents. Her parents have nothing to do with it." Her shoulders straightened and she thrust her chin out. With a commanding tone in her voice, she said, "You need to leave."

My eyes narrowed. "What? Mom, what's going to happen to her?"

"Mason, just go, go find Jack and have a nice weekend at the cabin." She patted my face. "You're done here. And I need to do my job." She turned to go out the door.

Looking back at the beautiful girl, I called after Mom, "Where are you going? You can't just leave her here."

Mom paused to look at the girl. "I have to go get someone." She took a quick breath. "And you need to not be here when we get back." She left.

The girl had quieted and was staring at me.

Black Sabbath blared from my cell phone.

Jack said, "I'm getting off a little early. I'll be at the end of the parking lot in about two minutes."

"Your two minutes always seem closer to ten."

"Two minutes, I swear. Just come out the same door you went in."

I stuffed the DVD into my backpack. "I have to go."

As if the girl cared, but I felt like I should explain.

"My mom will be back to . . ." I had no idea what would happen when my mom got back, or who she was bringing with her, or what it would mean for this strange, beautiful girl. But there was nothing I could do about it.

The girl stood up.

The top of her head cleared my chin, which meant she had to be close to six feet tall. And her athletic body looked taut, like she was ready for fight or flight. "We need to go. So the gardener doesn't find me."

Was she thinking about leaving with me? "Listen, I'm really sorry." She had no idea how sorry. "But I have to go."

I motioned toward the door. "My mom will be back any minute."

Before I could react, she turned and ran through the open door.

F O U R

"Wait!"

I followed the girl into the hall, where she had already disappeared through the fire door. As I went through the doorway, she pounded down the stairs, her flip-flops slapping on the stairs while I tried to keep up. "Hold on!" My voice echoed in the stairwell, way too loud.

As she descended, the girl looked more and more certain of her steps. She sure as hell didn't move like someone with a traumatic brain injury.

I tried to close the gap. She reached the emergency door, which opened to the sidewalk. Her hand reached out to push the silver bar, but then she turned and opened the door leading out of the stairwell and back inside.

A second later, I lunged through, bumping into her, righting myself just as I realized we were not alone.

A man dressed in a white orderly uniform had snagged the girl by the arm and held tight while she struggled. His name tag read Dennis. His eyes widened slightly as he noticed my scar, but his voice was gruff when he asked me, "What's this?"

I looked down for a second to catch my breath, wondering how I was going to get out of it.

"Steve?"

Was he talking to me? Then I realized I was still dressed the same as he was. Maybe I wasn't screwed. As I raised my head, I put a grin on my face. "Yeah, I'm . . . uh . . ." I tapped my name tag. "Steve. I'm Steve."

"Oh. Didn't know we had two Steves." Dennis glanced at the girl again.

"I'm new."

He rubbed his chin as he asked, "What floor she from?"

Took me a minute to remember. "Sixth."

Dennis looked at my backpack.

"I was just about ready to check out and then she took off running." Trying to play the part, I shook my head and swore.

"Believe it or not, that happens on the geezer floor, too, sometimes." He grinned. "But they're a little easier to catch." His eyes roamed to the girl's chest and farther down, then back up to her face. "She's a looker." Dennis licked his lips. "So you want me to take her back up?"

Yes! That was it. My out.

One word from me and I was out the door, off to the cabin. I could forget ever being at the Haven of Peace.

My mouth opened, but my breath caught in my throat. What was I doing? There was nothing I could do to help her. Was there? Maybe the bigger question was, did I want to be involved? Saving people was what I did. I wasn't one to back down, ever. But this situation involved my mom, to some degree. She was responsible for the girl. Did I truly think my mom wouldn't do the best thing for her?

My mind was saying, *Go, dude. Find Jack and leave.*

But my gut was saying something else. That something just wasn't right. That the girl did need saving. And I was the one to do it.

Her eyes were still on me, almost like she knew what I was thinking. Dennis the orderly still stared at the girl, a smarmy expression on his face that made me want to cringe. I allowed myself one more look.

Her brown eyes pleaded with me.

And it was those eyes that made me do what I did next. With one hand I reached out and held her firmly by the elbow. "No, I've got her."

With what seemed like an effort, Dennis took his eyes off her and released his grip. "Okay, big guy." He pointed at me. "Big Steve. That's the ticket. You're Big Steve. That's how we'll tell you two Steves apart." He gave me a little wave and headed down the hall.

I waited until he was out of sight, then pulled the girl through the door and outside as I muttered, "This is so dumb, this is so dumb, this is so dumb. . . ."

Still pulling the girl along, I ran down the sidewalk toward the parking lot. Two men dressed like me turned the corner, and I yanked her behind the hedge, where we crouched until they passed. But when I stood back up, I could see they were blocking our path to the sidewalk. "Perfect."

The girl frowned, then stepped over to the brick wall that bordered the back of the parking lot. "We need to climb over."

Even at my height, the top of the wall was nowhere near reachable. "How?"

She bent in front of me and made a cradle with her hands. "Step up."

"Oh, come on," I protested. "I've got at least a hundred pounds on you."

"Step up."

Just to prove my point, I lifted my foot and prepared to give her a little sample of my weight. But before I knew it, she'd hoisted me up like I was some tiny cheerleader.

I almost lost my balance and grabbed her shoulder as I planted a hand on the wall. "Whoa!"

"Grab the top of the wall and pull."

I didn't need to do much pulling, because she practically launched me up and over.

I had just dropped to the ground when her feet landed next to mine. The top of the wall seemed very far away. "How did you do that?"

She didn't answer.

I heard a vehicle approach and saw Jack pulling up.

Chilly rain dripped on us as we stood there. Her shirt was getting wet in spots.

"That's my ride."

She looked from the truck back to me. "I need a ride."

"Yeah, but—" But what? There was no use saying I wasn't involved. Yes, she had run from the sixth floor all on her own, but I became part of that escape the moment I took her from Dennis. Could I really just walk away and leave her standing in the parking lot?

Yes, I could. I had to.

Didn't I?

"Holy crap." So I ran to the truck, the girl right behind me. My hands trembled so much that it was difficult to open the door. The girl slid into the middle and I hopped in beside her and slammed the door.

Jack turned to me, mouth open. "They have babes working here?"

"Jack! Drive."

"Geez frickin' Louise." Jack shook his head, pulled out of the parking lot, and headed toward my house. "I work here all this time and don't meet anyone under the age of eighty, and you're here for, like, *twenty minutes* and—"

"She doesn't work there." I needed to tell him. "She's a patient on my mom's floor."

Jack slammed on the brakes and we jolted forward as far as the seat belts would give.

I probably should have waited until he was parked to tell him that. "Jack! Just keep driving."

He tromped on the accelerator and turned into the deserted parking lot of the Washington State Bank, then screeched to a stop. "She's a patient? You stole a patient?"

The girl watched Jack.

I tried to explain what happened on the sixth floor. "She took off and I followed and this orderly saw us. I couldn't just let her go back up there."

Jack's eyes were wide. "So what? You just what, figure, oh, I'll STEAL HER? What were you thinking?"

"I didn't steal her. She left first. I just chased her." My voice was quiet. "She wanted to go."

"Oh, great, Mace." Jack dropped his forehead onto the

steering wheel. "This is just great." When he lifted his head, his eyes blazed as he reached past the girl and stuck a finger in my chest. "You can't do this all the time! Be the frickin' hero! Some people aren't supposed to be saved. Some people can't be saved. Not by you, anyway."

I leaned away from him, resting my head on the cold window.

But his curiosity seemed to overcome his anger for a moment. "What's your name?"

"I don't know," the girl answered, rubbing her eyes as she peered out the windshield.

"Great," said Jack. "I suppose you don't know where you're from, either."

"I'm pretty sure I'm not from here."

Jack smacked the edge of the steering wheel with a fist. "God, Mace! You know how much trouble we're in?" He shook his head. "We're taking her back."

"And telling them what?"

I unbuckled and jumped out, stripping off the orderly uniform and rolling it into a ball, which I tossed behind the seat before climbing back in. "Jack, just go to my house. I'll call my mom, figure this out."

Jack's eyes narrowed and he said something not very nice under his breath.

"I mean, really, how are you going to explain all this? You snuck me in, gave me an orderly uniform, I steal a girl. . . ."

He put the truck in gear. "You suck."

The girl was quiet as we drove slowly through the town's

49

25 mph zone, but then she leaned over me and placed both palms on the window. "Those lights."

Distracted by the nearness of her, it took me a moment to follow her gaze.

Up on the hill above town, the lights from TroDyn illuminated the night sky with a bright glow. I said, "That's just a company that—"

She cut me off. "There's something familiar about them." She shook her head. "I'm just so . . . It feels like I have cobwebs in my head. I'm so fuzzy." The girl slapped both hands to her forehead. "Oh."

"What?" Jack glanced over at her, then back to the road. "What? What's wrong with her?"

At once, her head jerked back so that she stared straight up. Her eyes were wide as she spoke. One of her hands clutched at my shirt. "We've got to get away!"

Jack asked, "From where?"

Slowly, she turned to face the lights of TroDyn. "From there. We have to get away from there." And she started to rock back and forth, repeating, "We need to go, we need to go. . . ."

I held out a hand to touch her, do something, but I didn't know what, so I just put my hand back in my lap. "Jack, I think we should take her with us to the cabin."

His shook his head. "What? Are you nuts?"

I banged my head against the window a couple of times. "I know this is insane and you're pissed." My voice lowered. "But you weren't there, you didn't see them. I just couldn't leave her there." I had to convince him. Or at least say the right thing to get him on board, and I knew what that was. "It was like . . . destiny that I wake her up. I mean, what are the chances of me happening to play that DVD in the same room as her?"

He met my gaze and looked away.

As I waited for him to respond, the clock tower downtown struck the first few chords of nine o'clock.

Bong.

Bong.

Bong.

"Mace, are you screwing with me?" Jack's voice was drenched in doubt. As it should be, because I couldn't give a crap about destiny.

But, at that moment, I really needed him to think, to believe, that I did indeed give a crap. Because love, according to Jack, involved destiny. He got it from his mom, who met his dad only because she slid into a ditch on an icy night, and Jack's dad was the first person to come along and offer assistance. Plus, he was lost and not even supposed to be on that road. I'd heard the story about eighty times, so Jack must have really heard it a lot.

I shook my head. "No. I'm not screwing with you."

He bit his lip for a second. "You know how seriously I take destiny."

Yes, I knew. So I nodded. Furiously. "I'm being serious. Destiny. For sure."

"Well." Jack nodded a little bit, like he was thinking it over. "Okay. We'll go to the cabin." He looked at the girl and then at me. "But you still suck."

Jack headed south on I-5 toward Portland.

The girl seemed to be concentrating on holding her head and staving off voices or whatever it was she heard, then she gradually calmed the farther we got from Melby Falls. We connected with 84 East about an hour later, just as my cell phone rang. Mom was frantic, her voice a fast whisper. "Tell me you just left. Tell me you just left and you and Jack are on your way to the cabin. Tell me that."

It took me a minute to answer. "We are. We're on our way to the cabin right now."

"Really?"

"Yes, Mom. We just got on I-84. Why?"

She sighed. "No reason. Just . . . I . . . heard sirens, wanted to make sure you were okay."

She was lying; I could tell she was lying. "Something wrong, Mom?"

"No!" The word came too fast to be true. "No, it's fine. You and Jack have fun. Stay out of trouble."

The connection fizzed. "Mom?" I could hear only every other word. "Lost her!"

Jack leaned forward. "We're in the Gorge. Lousy coverage."

No point in wasting the battery, so I turned off my phone.

A few miles farther, Jack pointed at an exit sign with a Chevron symbol. "I need some gas." As we pulled in, I got out to fill the tank, but Jack motioned for me to stay put.

"This is Oregon," he said. "They have attendants for that."

So the girl stayed in the truck. Jack went inside and came back out carrying a plastic bag, which he handed to me.

I climbed back in as Jack started the truck. I was finally starting to relax and I couldn't do anything but think about the girl. Her smell, the way her leg felt pressed against mine, the sound of her voice. God, I finally find the perfect girl and she's a nutcase.

Jack reached over her and started rustling around in the bag.

"Just drive, I'll do that." I was hungry. "Did you get anything good?" I held up a Yoo-hoo. "Chocolate milk?"

The girl took it from me and cradled the bottle with both hands in her lap. Jack held out his hand and I found another Yoo-hoo for him.

I pulled out a can of Mountain Dew and opened it with a loud click. "Yes." The soda was icy. I took a big swig. "Ah. I needed that."

Jack tipped back his head and took a gulp of Yoo-hoo. "I haven't had this since I was a kid." He looked at her. "What about you?"

"I've never had it." She glanced down at the Yoo-hoo. "I like the colors."

And that was when Jack started whistling the theme from *The Twilight Zone.*

The rain came down harder as Jack steered onto the two-lane Bridge of the Gods across the Columbia River, and started up the mountain road toward Glenwood and the cabin. Jack and I chatted for a while, but it seemed we didn't have much practice acting normal in freakishly bizarre situations. So we pretty much rode in silence for most of the way.

As we reached Glenwood and drove through the deserted

streets, the girl still just held the chocolate milk and stared out the windshield into the night, the steady hum of the wipers the only sound.

The cabin was down the second right after the Glenwood Bed and Breakfast, and it was just a few minutes before we pulled into the yard of the cabin. Jack said, "Hit the garage opener, will you?"

I reached up for the shade. "It's not here."

Jack sighed and turned off the engine. We walked up the steps to the deck, where Jack tipped up an antique milk can and retrieved a key from underneath.

Inside, he flipped on all the lights.

The girl looked uncertain and I ushered her in. "It's okay. We're the only ones here."

She kept a tight grasp on her Yoo-hoo as we entered.

Jack's grandpa had made the cabin from old-growth timber. We walked into one huge room with a large kitchen, dining table, living room, and floor-to-ceiling fireplace made of Columbia River rocks.

I set the bag from the gas station on the table and headed over to pour water into the coffeemaker.

Along with destiny, Jack's family also believed in having the fire laid out in the fireplace, ready to go, and Jack soon had it roaring. He said, "I'm gonna go put the truck in the garage."

The girl stood in front of the fireplace, one hand outstretched toward the burning logs. The other still clutched the Yoo-hoo.

After a bit, the coffeemaker started to make slurping

sounds, and I pulled a cup out of the cupboard, then hunted for some kind of creamer.

Leaving the fireplace, the girl looked out the front picture window. Clouds started to break up, revealing the moon.

I felt like I should say something to try to put us both at ease. "There's a gorgeous view of Mount Adams. Sits right in the meadow." Yeah. That didn't work, because she didn't reply and I felt even more tense.

The half-and-half in the fridge was spoiled, so I poured it down the drain. I had to settle for powdered cream, which refused to dissolve entirely in my coffee.

"Looks like she's tired." Jack had come back in.

"Huh?"

He nodded at the girl.

She stood by the window, yawning.

I went over to her. "Do you want to get some sleep?" This seemed a funny thing to ask someone who recently came out of some freaked-up coma.

But her eyes drooped as she glanced over at Jack. "Here?"

Jack pointed down the hallway. "My sister's bedroom is down there." His older sister, Vanessa, was at Harvard. She wasn't as nice as Jack, but just as rich. And much better at taking standardized tests.

The girl nodded and looked at me. "Okay."

"I'll take you." I motioned to her Yoo-hoo. "Want me to put that in the fridge?"

She hesitated, then handed it to me, and I set it on the table.

Jack said, "There are some pajamas that'll fit you, I think.

And the bathroom is across the hall. There's all kinds of girl stuff in there; help yourself."

I led the way and the girl followed.

In the guest room, I turned on the light and pulled open a few drawers until I found a nightgown. It looked a bit short for her, but she took it anyway. There was a quilt on the end of the bed and several pillows. "You'll be okay?"

She sat on the very edge of the bed, barely touching it.

"Here." I spread the quilt over the bed, and then folded down the top. I threw all the pillows on the floor except for two, which I fluffed and lay on the head of the bed. "It's all ready for you to crawl in."

She didn't move.

"Okay. So just change and you'll be set."

Her eyes remained fixed on the garment in her lap, then they slowly raised to meet mine. "I'm not sure how."

The girl could throw me over a wall, but she couldn't get dressed?

She stammered a little. "I mean, there are so many things swirling in my head, and it's like I have to reach up and catch them in order to use them. But the one about getting dressed, it's just not . . . letting me grab ahold."

"Well, you just take those clothes off and put that on." I pointed at the nightgown.

She looked so helpless sitting there.

I rubbed my eyes a bit. "Okay. Just . . . turn around."

She stood up and turned around to face the window.

Stepping in close behind her, I tried to ignore the fact that I was living some amazing fantasy, and instead focused on my latent leadership skills. "Put your arms straight up." This wasn't exactly how I'd imagined my first time undressing a girl.

She lifted her arms toward the ceiling.

I gingerly grasped the hem of her shirt, a little fearful I might make some wrong move that would cause her to heave me through the wall. Averting my head so I couldn't see anything, I lifted it off. I instructed, "Okay, now put the nightgown on." I couldn't resist sneaking a brief glimpse of her sinewy bare back.

She struggled a little but managed to get the nightgown over her head. Then her arms got stuck and I yanked a bit until it drifted down, the bottom coming to just above the knees of her red sweatpants.

"And when I leave, you can just, um, take off your sweats and you're all set."

She turned around so that we were just inches apart.

I stepped back.

She almost smiled. "I've got it now." Before I could look away, she dropped her sweats, but the nightgown covered anything I shouldn't have seen anyway. "I'll sleep now."

Walking backward toward the door, I said, with a little too much cheer, "Good! Fine, I'll just get the lights—"

As she started to climb into bed, her short nightgown revealed the back of her legs from the knee down. And I tried not to keep from gasping at the circular scars that covered the entire length of them.

FIVE

I'D NEVER SEEN SUCH GNARLED, NASTY SCARS. AND SHE thought *I* was marked. Then, as the most beautiful girl I'd ever seen settled into the bed, she stared at me. Like she was waiting for something.

From me.

With one large step, I was at the bedside.

After pausing for just a second, I tugged the quilt up to her chin, said good night, and flipped out the light. Then I stepped out in the hall, shut the door, and leaned back against it, my heart threatening to burst out of my chest at any moment.

In the other room, Jack ate pretzels from a blue bowl. He shoved them my way as I sat down. "Sorry, not much food. I'll get more in the morning. What's the plan, Mace?"

Grabbing a handful of pretzels, I shook my head. "No clue."

"That was kind of weird how she freaked out when she saw TroDyn."

I nodded as I chewed. "Maybe her parents work there or something."

Jack grinned. "Maybe she was forced to do a summer internship there, and it fried her brain."

"Funny. She just came out of a coma or something. She probably would've freaked out at lights of the nearest Seven-Eleven." I sounded like I was trying to convince myself of something.

Jack frowned.

I swallowed. "What?"

"It's just weird." Jack shrugged. "I don't know. TroDyn owns the nursing home."

"So?" I didn't get what that had to do with anything. "They also own most of the town."

Jack leaned forward. "Don't take this the wrong way. But your mom has this mystery history with TroDyn, and now she works at the Haven?" He jabbed his thumb toward the hallway. "And this girl is there and then gets all *run, Toto, run* when she sees the lights of TroDyn."

I shoved another handful of pretzels in my mouth so I didn't have to answer. There was no way my mom was involved with that girl any more than taking her vitals every half hour. And, obviously, she had instructions to call somebody if the girl, or the others, ever woke up. It seemed my mom did have some kind of history with TroDyn, but it was over. She didn't work at the labs anymore. "There's nothing there. My mom doesn't know who this girl is any more than we do." Again with the trying to convince myself.

"Still," said Jack. "I had no idea there was anyone but old people at the Haven. That kind of pisses me off."

"Jack, TroDyn has been part of our lives forever. I'm trying to make it part of my future." But I was curious. "Maybe

TroDyn is doing research with accident victims, trying to cure their amnesia. Which would explain a lot."

Jack nodded. "It's easy enough to look up. Maybe she's just afraid because she doesn't remember who she is."

Although I had no idea what he thought he would find, I grabbed my coffee and followed Jack into the office, just down the hall from Vanessa's room, where the girl slept. I guess I wanted to be there when he discovered exactly what I knew he would: nothing.

Jack started to open the connection while I set my cup down and flopped into a leather recliner alongside a tall shelf of books. My eyes started to get heavy.

"Mace."

"Huh?" My mouth tasted scummy. "Did I fall asleep?"

"Duh." Jack pointed at the clock.

I'd been asleep for two hours. "You've been online the whole time?"

"Took me forever. Dial-up sucks." He held up a stack of paper and flipped a few pages around.

I rubbed my eyes. "What's that?"

"Funny you should ask. TroDyn is very public about their research that pertains to global warming and environmental sustainability. Like, full disclosure. Their scientists publish in all the journals."

"Yeah, I know all that." I had to write a paper to go with my application.

"That's not the issue," said Jack.

"There's an issue?"

Jack asked, "Where's the best place to hide?"

I thought about the discovery when I was ten that Mom kept all my Christmas presents on top of the fridge in a brown paper grocery bag labeled COUPONS. "In plain sight?"

"Exactly." Jack held up a printout of a newspaper clipping. "TroDyn is always on the up and up, always flooding the media with massive amounts of information, so much so that it's more than any journals or newspapers would ever want or need to publish. TroDyn overkill. So they never have anyone knocking on their door. The media is already saturated with TroDyn."

I stretched and yawned. "So, it's what they're *not* telling the public?"

Jack nodded. "Looks that way. And get this, not many scientists have left TroDyn, but some have."

"And?"

"Dude, this is the frickin' weird part. There are some serious similarities. Listen to this." He took a sip of coffee before reading out loud, "Donald Andreason, scientist for seven years with TroDyn before starting his own consulting firm, had this to say about his former employer: 'While my time with TroDyn was enriching to my career, I ultimately decided my best career options lay in another direction, and they amicably accepted my resignation, wishing me well in my new endeavor.'"

I didn't see what was so weird about that, until Jack read from another sheet of paper. "Jessica Lee, scientist for six years with TroDyn, recently left to take an academic position at USC. Of her former employer, she had these words: 'While my time with TroDyn was enriching to my career, I ultimately decided my best career options lay in another direction, and they amicably accepted my resignation, wishing me well in my new endeavor.'"

"It's the same."

"Exactly." Jack set the papers on the desk. "Like a piece TroDyn required its former employees to memorize. And here's another thing." He tapped the computer screen. "In the twenty-two years TroDyn has been in Melby Falls, there has been a total of thirty-one employees who left TroDyn for various new jobs. They all had the same words for their former employer, and except for one, they all had something else in common."

"What?"

Jack tapped the desk. "Each had their first child born within seven months of leaving TroDyn."

I didn't get it. "They left because they were having a baby?"

Jack said, "Or in the case of the men, their wives were."

"This is really weird." And if it involved the girl, the whole thing was way too weird for me and Jack to handle on our own.

He asked, "You thinking what I'm thinking?"

I said, "We need to take her back?"

Jack took a sip of his coffee. "The destiny stuff was a load of bull, wasn't it?"

"Sorry. I just really wanted to help her."

He nodded. "I get it."

"I should have let you turn around and take her back." I sighed. "First thing tomorrow?"

"Yeah," he said. "Let's get some sleep. And maybe we can think up some great story to tell my boss that won't get me fired or put us both in juvie."

Just then, we heard a noise.

"Was that her?" asked Jack.

"I think so. I'll go." I stopped at the bathroom and dug until I found some Scope, then swished for a few seconds before tiptoeing to her door. My rapping knuckles on the wood sounded like thunder. "Hello?"

"Please."

I turned the knob and pushed.

She was upright in bed, staring out at the moon.

Taking a few steps into the room, I asked, "Are you okay?"

She turned to me. "I can't really hear them anymore."

"Who?"

Her knees bunched up and she dropped her head onto them, then started rocking forward and back. "It hurts, it hurts."

I went over and sat on the edge of the bed. One of my hands went out to touch her, but it hovered there in the space between us before I pulled back. "What hurts?"

"My head. It hurts without them there. It's so empty." She turned her face to me. "I want some light."

I pulled the string on the lamp. Her eyes were wide in the sudden glare and she shrank back from me.

I froze. "Did I scare you?" My face had certainly frightened people before, it wasn't anything new.

But she shook her head. "I think I just adjust slowly. To new things."

I picked at a loose thread on the bottom of my shirt for a moment, not sure what to say. Then I figured, I might as well ask what I wanted to. "Can you tell me about where you're from?"

She tilted her head to the left as her eyes looked right. Ask someone a multiplication problem that they have to do in their head, they will look left. Asked for something they already know but have to recall, they will inevitably look right. So I knew she was remembering. Or at least trying to.

"I was in the seventh row from the back, third from the end."

"At the Haven?" I didn't get it. "You were all just on a couch together."

"No." She looked down again, maybe remembering more. When she raised her head again, her voice was firmer, like she was more certain of the truth of what she was saying. "Before the Haven, in the place before. I was in the seventh row from the back, third from the end."

I swallowed, wanting to ask her what she was talking about but afraid she might stop speaking if I interrupted.

Her eyes glazed a little as she continued her story. "Our position didn't matter. Our state of being was identical. Calmness and serenity, all shared as one." She smiled a little as she placed a hand on her chest. "We knew only peace and comfort."

Her forehead wrinkled a little. "I was . . . we were . . . content. There was no fear or sorrow. But . . ."

I waited for her to go on, which she did, after a deep breath. "We breathed as one. We moved as one." She closed her eyes. "We thought as one." And then it was almost as if she heard chanting in her head, which she had to join. "There will be no weakness." Her eyes shot open, widening at her words. "It's time. I feel it."

I couldn't help myself as I asked, "Feel what?"

"The one nearest the door. He shivers first, and that slight tremble trickles down row after row, space after space. It hits me." Her head lowers slightly. "I shiver in response. That is how I know."

I whispered, "Know what?"

She swallowed. "That was how I knew the Gardener was coming."

Her eyes widened and she clutched my shirt with one hand, pulling me toward her.

I tried to ignore the fact that her face was so close I felt her warm breath on my own face. "You remembered."

She bit her bottom lip for a second. "But it wasn't complete, just a glimpse."

Her lips were perfect and I could have stared at them forever. But I made myself go back to her eyes. "Maybe you need time to remember the rest?" But I didn't want her to need more time. I wanted to know more immediately. I wanted her to remember it all, tell me everything about herself.

"Maybe." She nodded as she released her grip on my shirt and reached for my hand, holding on.

Her hand in my mine was soft and warm. Her nails were medium length, nicely clipped. Upon closer inspection, I noticed that partway down, each white tip had a line of a different color white, like a tree has rings. I'd seen that once before, on my mom's nails when she got really sick with a virus. That white line was an indicator to me that in the recent past, this girl had suffered something physically traumatic. I wondered if it had anything to do with the scars on her legs.

I met her gaze. There was so much more I wanted to ask her, but she looked exhausted. So I said, "You should really try and sleep more."

She blinked a few times, then lay back, still holding my hand. "Will you stay?"

"Do you want me to?"

"Yes." And she shut her eyes.

I leaned forward to turn out the light, but her eyes popped open and she squeezed my hand. "Leave it on. I don't like the dark."

"Okay." Still holding her hand, I slipped down onto the floor and laid my head on the bed, just looking at her profile. Her grip was still strong. I'd never held a girl's hand before.

Part of me was jumping up and down happy that somehow I could make this strange lovely girl feel protected. But I didn't know if I was her protector or her kidnapper. Was her story about the place before the Haven true? Did anyone else know? Part of me wanted to call my mom, make her tell me everything she knew about the girl.

But another part didn't want to know any more. As long as I was a little ignorant of reality, I could enjoy the present moment. As soon as reality infringed on that, even one fact about who she was or who might be looking for her or how much trouble I was in, my little fantasy moment would shatter. Maybe there was a connection between this girl and TroDyn, or maybe Jack and I were being paranoid. In the morning, we'd take her back and that would be it.

Her hand pulled on mine. "You can sleep up here."

I didn't argue.

Sliding up on the bed, I kept one foot on the floor. But then she slid over and patted the space beside her. Still under the covers, she rolled away from me but pulled my hand with her, so that I ended up curled against her back, the bulky covers between us, one of my arms around her and the other arm under my head. Leaning forward just slightly, my face was in her hair and I inhaled. I asked, "Did you remember your name?"

She didn't answer at first. Then I felt her shake her head no. "Does it matter?"

"No," I lied.

Soon her breathing slowed and steadied itself. My eyes shut, but there was no way I would be able to sleep, lying so close to her. Still, I wouldn't want to miss a moment of it. I wished I knew her name.

When Jack woke me up, I was facing away from her, my head on the edge of the bed, my face in drool.

He raised one thumb and both eyebrows.

I flipped him off.

Quickly, I sat up and wiped my face on my sleeve. The girl was still asleep.

In the kitchen, there was a fresh pot of coffee. I poured myself a cup and joined Jack at the table.

He had a huge grin on his face. "Dude!"

"Shut up, Jack. She just wanted me to sleep with her." I scrunched my eyes shut as I realized how that sounded.

He whistled.

"No, just sleep. Believe me." I squinted at the clock on the stove, but the digital numbers blurred. "What time is it?"

Jack yawned. "About nine."

I stirred in some powdered creamer and asked, "Why *did* you interrupt my perfect moment, anyway?"

"I was lonely." Jack grinned. "No, I'm gonna run to the gas station for some juice and donuts. Then we probably should get her back." He played catch with his keys on his way to the door.

"Get some real cream, too," I called after him. Taking my coffee with white creamer clumps into the living room, I stretched out on the couch and grabbed the remote. The satellite showed about a billion channels, but it seemed like the only things on at that hour were cartoons, infomercials, or news programs.

I was surfing past some woman being interviewed when an item in the bullet list on the screen caught my eye.

Former TroDyn Scientist

I turned up the sound. Her name was Dr. Kelly Emerson. I learned she'd been a researcher at TroDyn for several years before starting her own environmental consulting firm. She'd ended up on several presidential committees concerning global warming and was talking about a book she'd written involving the future of food, and the potential adaptation of species to global warming. Survival of the fittest.

I was disappointed to see the interviewer asked her nothing about TroDyn until the very end. She seemed a little annoyed that the subject got brought up, but her pat reply was no surprise.

"While my time with TroDyn was enriching to my career, I ultimately decided my best career options lay in another direction, and they amicably accepted my resignation, wishing me well in my new endeavor."

After that, TroDyn wasn't mentioned again.

I clicked the television off just as Jack returned with small containers of cream and blue packets of sweetener and a plastic tub of powdered-sugar donuts. Jack bit into a donut. His mouth full, he said, "We have a little problem."

Reaching over him, I plucked a donut from the tub and bit into it. "What?"

"When I went into the gas station, there was some guy in a suit asking Lucille questions about a red truck." Lucille was an older lady who not only owned the gas station but kept an eye on the cabin for Jack's parents.

"Yours?" I shoved the rest of the donut in my mouth and chewed.

"Well, I hid behind the chips before he saw me, but then when he went outside, he stood by the truck for a while, talking on his cell phone."

"What did he do when you went back out?"

He shook his head as he took another bite of donut. "I didn't. Lucille sent me out the back and had her husband give me a lift. I left the truck there."

"Maybe he was some angry husband looking for his wife and she has a red truck? Besides, if someone was looking for us, how would they know we were here?"

Jack shrugged. "It was dark when we got into town. Even Lucille was surprised to see me, and she's the town gossip. If she doesn't know something, no one does."

"Do you think someone from Melby Falls knows we have her?" I tapped my fist against my lips. "How?"

His forehead wrinkled. "There are security cameras in the parking lot at Haven of Peace."

I almost spit out my coffee. "Then they probably have it on tape."

"About that," said Jack. "You know, the THEY part? I have a feeling we're not talking about my supervisor, Suzy, in the geezer ward."

"No." I shook my head. "Doubtful. But do you want to wait around to find out? I mean, isn't this considered kidnapping?"

Jack tilted his head. "Mace, did you carry her out of the building, kicking and screaming?"

It was almost the opposite, actually. "Definitely not."

Jack scratched his chin. "We'll take her back, no harm done. It's not like someone is going to knock on the door in the next five minutes." But his eyes flicked to the door as if that was exactly what he expected to happen, which made me nervous.

So I rationalized out loud, my words coming a little faster than usual. "Okay, so what do we know? Facts, all of them." I started at the beginning. "She was in the nursing home and somehow the words in the DVD woke her up. And she was confused. Scared maybe. Definitely scared when she started ranting about the gardener."

Jack's words also were rushed. "But that's just part of the story, right? Maybe it's like when you fall asleep with the television on and then pretty soon the ten o'clock newscaster is in your dream."

That made sense. "Maybe," I said. "Maybe." But then there was the rest. "But she threw me over the wall, Jack. That makes no sense at all."

Jack pursed his lips and looked like he was thinking. "So we have a girl who was catatonic but woke up because of a children's book. She freaks out and throws a sizable offensive tackle over a wall."

The events of the night before ran through my head in order. "Then she held a bottle of Yoo-hoo for three hours before going to sleep for the night."

Jack started to pace. "And it was so weird that she freaked out when she saw the lights of TroDyn."

Nodding in agreement, I wanted to add something else to the list of bizarreness circling the girl. The scars on her legs. But when I opened my mouth to tell him, I shut it again. For some reason, it didn't seem right to spill that. Or the story she had told me, which was probably just some strange dream she had, anyway.

"Man, it's just all weird." Jack sat down and leaned back, putting the chair on two legs. "Well, once I get my truck back, you'll have a three-hour ride to find out what is going on with this girl."

"Maybe even her name," I said hopefully.

Just then, she walked into the room.

I stood up while Jack dropped the chair back onto four legs with a bam.

Her eyes met mine and she almost smiled.

"Good morning," I said. "Sleep okay?"

"Yes." She seemed much more clearheaded as she looked around. "But . . . I hurt here." She held her stomach, and at that moment, it growled so loud we all heard it.

Jack grinned. "I would hazard a guess and say you're hungry."

Her forehead creased.

Walking toward her, I held out my hand. It was like I was dealing with a wild kitten, trying to keep her from running off.

"You need to eat," I said, as she put her hand in mine. "You do remember eating?"

She looked at the donuts on the table.

I led her to the table, and she sat down.

"Here." Jack put a few donuts on a napkin and handed them to her.

The girl watched Jack shove another donut into his mouth and she copied him, the donut disappearing into her mouth as her cheeks puffed up and she started to chew. Powdered sugar spilled out of her mouth.

Jack stared openmouthed and I realized I was doing the same.

I pushed a napkin over toward her as she struggled to keep the donut in. "Jack, I think you've met your match."

She swallowed. Then her eyes widened and started to water as her hand went over her mouth.

Jack shook a hand toward the sliding glass door onto the back deck. "Get her out, get her out! My mom'll kill me if someone pukes in here."

I grabbed her and led her over to the door. Outside, she doubled over and threw up every bite she'd just eaten onto the wet grass.

"Wait here." Inside, I grabbed a few napkins, which I took back outside and handed to her.

She wiped her mouth, then straightened up.

Trying not to stare at her, I looked off toward Mount Adams, except that all the clouds and rain pretty much made it invisible. I asked, "Is that another thing you can't grab ahold of? Eating?"

She stepped closer to me but didn't say anything.

Facing her again, I lowered my voice. "It's okay. I haven't told Jack about that."

The corner of her mouth went up. "Thanks."

"Listen . . ." I wasn't sure how to tell her that she was going back, that I'd be dumping her off at the same place she wanted so desperately to get away from.

In a flash, her hand reached out and squeezed my arm.

She cocked her head to one side, then slowly straightened it. "They're here."

Chills went down my spine at the tone of her voice. "Who's here?"

She turned and walked to the end of the deck and looked toward the end of the driveway, where the large gate blocked the view of the road. She pointed. "There. They're waiting out there."

We went back inside, my words running together. "Jack, have you got some binoculars?"

He frowned. "What's wrong?"

"Just show me!"

Jack shook his head. "No binocs, but my mom's birding scope is in the closet by the laundry room."

As I headed that way, he called, "It cost a ton! Be careful."

I found it. "Got a ladder?"

Jack nodded. "What are you doing?"

"I need to check the front gate."

Jack made an odd face. "So walk out and check the front gate."

"I can't." I pointed. "There's someone out there and I don't want them to see me."

He flapped a hand skyward. "So go up on the roof."

I handed him the scope. "Duh. That's why I need a ladder."

Outside, there was a slight mist coming down. Jack carried the scope and helped me get the ladder, then climbed up behind me to the edge of the roof. We both shimmied our way up the damp, scratchy, black shingles to the peak,

then peered over. A black sedan sat on the opposite side of the road from the gate.

Jack looked through the scope first, then blew out a breath. "That's the guy from the gas station."

"You sure?"

He nodded.

I looked next. "Someone's in the backseat. Looks like a couple of people."

Jack said, "Maybe it's orderlies. Or cops. If they came ready to take her back."

"Cops would knock on the door, wouldn't they?" The view wasn't close enough to see. I asked, "Does this zoom?"

While I looked through, Jack turned a knob on the scope, and the occupants of the backseat got bigger and came into focus. I sucked in a quick breath. The people in the backseat weren't orderlies. Or cops.

The three people in the backseat were the kids I'd seen sitting next to the girl at Haven of Peace. I breathed out a four-letter word my mother would have slapped me for. What were they doing there? Why? And if they were there, where was my mom? Was she okay?

"What?" Jack asked. "Who is it?"

The girl had been right. They *were* here.

I handed the scope back to Jack and motioned for him to climb down. "I've seen them before. They're the others from the sixth floor at the Haven of Peace." My hands started to tremble. "They've come looking for her."

"Maybe he's her dad," Jack said. "Do we hand her over?"

Did we just hand her over? I didn't believe for a second

that the guy at the front gate was her dad or anything as simple as that. My gut was screaming the opposite. I looked at Jack. "There's no way I'm letting her go back there."

Jack dropped his head onto his hands. "Oh, man. What did you get us into?"

SIX

BACK INSIDE, THE GIRL SAT QUIETLY ON THE COUCH.

"I have an idea." Jack headed into the kitchen and made a call from the phone. He said a few words, then came back in, clicking it shut. "Get her dressed, something warm. Then meet me in the CC."

Hoping Jack's idea was better than the big pile of no ideas rambling around my head, I went down the hall to Vanessa's room. I dug through some drawers until I found a pair of jeans and a pink cable-knit sweater that looked about the girl's size. Jack's sister was shorter but tended to wear her pants way too long anyway. Leaving the outfit the girl had arrived in where it lay on the floor, I carried the other things out to her.

She took them and disappeared into the bathroom. I guess she was remembering how to do things.

Jack was in the CC, which stood for the Columbia Closet. It actually was a closet, but so huge, well lighted, and stocked, it could have been its own Columbia retail store, for all the gear it held. Jack's family liked convenience. So rather than hauling clothes and stuff back and forth to the cabin, they simply bought a ton of outdoor gear: coats for all seasons, boots, footwear, hats, gloves, enough for them and their guests. Jack had christened it the CC.

He handed me a pink jacket.

I held it up. "Not my color, dude."

"It's for her. You can get your own stuff."

I grabbed an XXL blue waterproof coat with a polar fleece lining, and gloves for the girl. I had worn my hiking boots, luckily, and I found a pair of Jack's that might work for her. Taking my haul out to the living room, I dumped it all on the floor just as she came out of the bathroom. Wearing jeans, the sweater, and her flip-flops, she looked like most of the girls at our high school.

Except way more beautiful than any of them.

She was so stunning just standing there that it took me a second to speak as I tried to convince myself that this gorgeous creature had actually asked me to hold her all night. I managed to spit out, "You'll want some socks." I held up the boots. "And these will be a little better than the flip-flops."

The girl asked, "Are we going outside?"

"Yep." Jack walked in. "And we're not going out the front gate."

Putting on my coat, I wondered what his plan was, but he kept talking.

"Lucille's place is about three miles through the trails. We can take the ATVs and then borrow her old Dodge truck. She used to let me drive it before I had my license." When I raised my eyebrows, he grinned. "My dad pays her

78

for watching out for the place. Which is why she drives a Cadillac now and not the old Dodge."

Running the trails through my mind, I tried to picture where Lucille's was. And the only image that came to mind was a house up on the ridge at the end of the trail we had named after Lewis and Clark. Mainly because we'd blazed it ourselves and it was the roughest of them all. "Jack, which trail?"

He donned a black jacket and zipped. "Lewis and Clark."

Not the best of news. "That's gonna be a mess with all this rain."

He nodded. "We'll go slow."

When I just looked at him, he held his hands up and let them drop. "Do we have a choice?"

No. I was pretty sure we didn't, and I shook my head. But then I said, "Are we nuts? What if we just call the police, explain it all?"

The girl touched my arm. "Would they help me? What would they do?"

I didn't know. "You'd probably go back to Haven of Peace."

Her light touch became a strong grip. "Don't make me go back there. Please, I'll go wherever we need to go."

"It's okay." I rested a hand on hers until she loosened her grip. "But can you tell me about the people out there? I mean, they were with you on the couch at the Haven of Peace." What I really wanted to know was, was the dark-haired boy a friend? More than a friend? Did she want to go to him?

"I don't remember any of that. And I don't feel . . . scared exactly. I can feel them, hear them. But I don't want to go out there."

"That's settled." Jack clapped his hands, startling me. "Let's saddle up, people."

Jack's mom was pretty adamant about keeping the ATVs, and accompanying noise, away from the house. So the shed housing all the Arctic Cats was a few hundred yards behind the house, toward the meadow and, luckily, away from the front gate.

The mist had turned into drizzle. Jack and I put our hoods up for the walk. The girl hadn't seemed to figure it out, so I stepped in front of her. "Wait." Reaching out, I pulled her hood up to cover her head. "Better?"

She nodded.

Jack unlocked the side door of the shed and we all went inside. With the lights flipped on, the place looked like a mini showroom for an ATV dealer. I went to one of the two red ones nearest the door. Jack handed us helmets and I pulled mine over my head, then helped the girl with hers. Her big eyes shone out and I wondered what she was thinking.

I flipped my leg over and took a seat on the machine. "You'll have to ride behind me. Can you hold on?"

Her hands clenched my shoulders as she climbed on behind me, the lack of room causing her to nestle right into my back. Not that I minded. Her body molding to mine was like a mirror image of the night before, when I had held her. An experience I could get used to.

Jack rolled up the big door and I turned the key. The ATV came to life under us, and the girl's arms quickly went around my waist, squeezing. In that moment I realized that starting the engine was a kind of point of no return. Turning that key was a conscious choice, a choice to not take the girl back.

I put one hand on her arm and turned my head to the side so she could hear. "You okay?"

"Yes!" Her voice was right at my ear.

As we moved forward out the door, I hoped I would be able to protect her.

Jack followed with a machine, then went back inside, disappeared behind the door as it lowered, then showed up a minute later. "Ready?"

I nodded.

He led the way across the meadow and into the start of the forest.

The girl held fast to my waist as I gripped the handles, staying far enough behind Jack to stop if he did. Our engines seemed so loud that I worried they'd alert the guy at the front gate. But all we could do was go, move away from there, and cross our fingers that our exit was as quiet as we hoped.

Concentrating as we started going up toward the slick trail, I was pretty sure we'd be okay as long as we went slow. The biggest danger lay in the unexpected—a fallen tree, or if part of the trail had washed out.

Still, despite the strangeness of the day, not to mention the danger of the moment, the grin on my face was automatic. I loved being on the machine, the roughness of the ride. I could have done without the wet and chilly day, but it was the Northwest; more often than not we had rain when we rode the ATVs.

As we climbed and angled upward, trees grew scarcer on our right until they disappeared completely and were replaced by a drop-off into a sizable chasm, lush with vegetation. The girl tightened her hold on me. Turning my head, I called back, "It's okay, I'll stay to the other side." She didn't say anything, but she did lay her head against my back, tucking in even closer than she had been.

Maybe it was being distracted by her that made me react slower when Jack's ATV started slipping on the muddy path. Just as I noticed he was having trouble, he started to slide backward, and I couldn't do anything other than try to turn as I hit the brakes, way too late.

His ATV bumped into mine, but the heavier weight and speed of my machine spun him halfway around and pushed him to the right toward the chasm.

"Jack!"

Flipping the key, I was off the ATV before the engine even died, lunging toward the edge, managing to catch the front fender of Jack's ATV just as his back wheels went over the edge.

In a squat, I had next to no leverage, just whatever strength I could summon to hold on. But I started to slide, and Jack and the front wheels of the ATV crept closer and closer to the edge.

Then arms went around my middle, pulling me back.

The girl.

But she only pulled like a normal person, not the person who had thrown me over the wall. There wasn't time to wonder where her strength went, because although my slide slowed, I still headed toward the edge.

Jack was nearly tipped back flat, hanging on to the ATV so as not to fall off. If I let go to try and help him get off and back to the edge, the ATV would plummet before I had a chance. And if the girl let go of me to help him, I'd go sliding over with him.

Jack was yelling, "Don't let go! Don't let go!"

"Jack! Hang on!"

A tree root off to my left looked strong. "Try to aim toward that!" With the girl shifting, I succeeded in planting one foot there. The girl still had her arms around my waist.

I knew I couldn't hold on much longer to the slippery fender.

Jack was still yelling, although I wasn't sure it was even words anymore.

Although I squeezed until it hurt, I felt the machine slipping away. "No!" I pushed on the tree root with everything I had.

But my fingers gave out and the ATV, along with my best friend, slipped out of my grasp.

The release sent me falling backward into the muck on

top of the girl. Rolling off, I scrambled to the edge, where I still heard crashing in the trees. I ripped off my helmet so I could see better.

The foliage was so thick and the light so gray and foggy, I couldn't see Jack or the ATV.

The crashing stopped. I heard only the rain and a few birds.

"Do you see him?" The girl looked with me.

"No. Stay here." I started down the side, grabbing for trees to hold on to as I slipped in the mud. "Jack!" I followed the path of broken tree branches. "Please be okay, please be okay." I kept screaming his name until finally I saw a bit of red at the bottom of the ravine.

I froze, trying not to breathe, and listened.

Nothing.

I ran toward the red and found Jack lying at the bottom of the chasm under the ATV. "Jack!"

His eyes were shut beneath the helmet. "Jack! Jack!" Another moment flashed before me, only I was the one lying on the ground hurt. And in that moment I had just a small idea of how my mother must have felt seeing me so still, my face half ripped off.

Jack didn't move and I slowly pulled off his helmet and touched his face. "Jack. Jack!" I shut my eyes and dropped my ear to his chest, listening for a heartbeat.

"Please be okay."

SEVEN

I couldn't hear Jack's heartbeat over my own.

He didn't move for so long. Then there was a low groan.

I sat back up. "Jack! Thank god!" My head dropped to his side and I let it rest there for a moment.

Jack said, "I'm fine."

I started to pull on his arm and he screamed.

"Sorry sorry sorry!"

"I take that back." Jack moaned. "I may not be fine, but I'm alive. And if I can feel all my injuries, that's good, right?"

Getting to my feet, I kicked at the ATV. "I'm gonna get you out. Do you think I can pull this off without hurting you?"

He seemed to be taking a mental inventory, then nodded. "I don't think any body parts are tangled."

Grasping an edge of the ATV, I started to lift it up and over, going very slowly. He didn't say anything as I finished and gave the machine a final shove so it landed upright, bouncing on its wheels as it righted itself. Kneeling beside him, I looked him over. "What's hurt?"

He bit his lip and winced as he tried to move. "My shoulder's dislocated again." By again, he meant for the fifth time. The first was when we were in grade school. Saturday morning basketball; I was dribbling forward while he guarded me, and he tripped over himself, smashing backward to the floor.

Back then, he was my ride home, so I had to go to the ER with him and his mother and sit out in the waiting room. I still remember his sobs, and then a scream. He came out all red-faced and sniffling, his arm in a sling.

The second time was during the first football practice freshman year. Jack took one hit and lay writhing on the ground until the team trainer walked over, grabbed his arm, and before Jack could utter a sound, snapped it back in place. Jack got up, walked off the field, and never came back.

After the third, a freakish paper route incident, and fourth, which involved homecoming, cheerleaders, and a pie-eating contest gone awry, he'd become a bit of a bragger about it. So when he lay there with foliage around his head, looking up at me and raising his eyebrows, I shook my head. "No frickin' way. I'm not doing it."

"Mace, come on." Jack pointed at his shoulder. "Just snap it back in, then I'm good to go."

"No." I sat down on the wet, muddy ground.

Jack said, "So we're just going to sit here."

"No." Although I wasn't sure how to get him up the hill with that shoulder.

"Seriously, it's easy. Last time at the pep rally, it took the cheerleading coach, like, three seconds. And she weighs the same as your left thigh."

Slapping my hands over my face, I groaned. "I can't believe I'm doing this."

"Dude, you're strong, it'll be cake."

"Fine." I dropped my hands and got up on my knees. "What do I do?"

He looked at my coat. "Stick some of that down under my armpit, to pad it."

Removing my coat, I folded up a sleeve and carefully placed it in his armpit. "Why do I need to pad that?"

"Because that's where your foot goes."

"Huh?" I backed off. "No way."

"Come on, man! You can do this. I'm the one in pain and you're being a wuss."

Jack was right.

I breathed out. "Fine, just tell me what to do."

"You're gonna put a foot in my armpit, then hold my hand."

I did as he said. With my foot in his armpit, I held his hand with one of mine, and gripped his arm with the other.

"Now, when I say so, you're going to slightly push with your foot as you really gently, and I am stressing the *really gently*, pull my arm." He rolled his head to the side and covered his eyes with his good arm.

"What's wrong?"

He didn't move, just said, "I'm not gonna watch, stupid."

"Okay. Let me know when you're ready."

"Okay." He took a couple of deep breaths. "No, wait!"

"What?"

"Remember, I said really gently."

I breathed out, gearing up. "Yeah, I heard you."

As Jack started to reply, I pushed with my foot as I pulled on his arm. With a grisly twinge, and a scream from Jack, the shoulder went back into place.

At the same time, we both swore.

Jack dropped his good arm to look at his bad one. "It's in. Good job."

"So we can try and get up the hill."

"About that," Jack said. "My right leg hurts like hell. Just the lower part, though."

Reaching down, I gently lifted up the bottom of his jeans. The lower part of his leg was already purple. I didn't know for sure, but I had the feeling it might be broken. At least there was no bone sticking out. Quickly, I lowered the pant leg without letting him know what I saw. Looking back the way I'd come, I rubbed my chin. "I'm gonna have to carry you up."

"Maybe I can walk." He started to move and grimaced.

"You can't walk."

He rolled his eyes. "Well, you can't carry me."

Sitting back on my haunches, I put both hands on the ground beside me. "Jack, I can bench two hundred. I think I can carry your scrawny ass up a hill."

He started to laugh, then winced. "Just watch the shoulder. They usually put it in a sling."

I pulled off my sweatshirt and put a makeshift sling over his coat. Not pretty, but it would work until the real thing.

My coat was all muddy, but I put it back on, anyway. Just that little while without it had chilled me in the damp air.

He said, "Get on that side."

As I maneuvered to get him into a cradle hold, he directed me about what parts of his body to avoid. With his sling to the outside, I managed to stand up with him in my arms.

"If you tell anyone you carried me like a girl, you are dead to me."

Ignoring him, worrying about whether I could indeed make it up that hill with him in my arms, I started climbing. The tricky part was making sure I had solid footing before taking another step. After a few minutes, I was breathing hard, and after about ten, I had to stop and lean against a tree.

"You can put me down, you know."

I shook my head, doubting I could pick him up again once I put him down. "I need a little breather is all. Here we go."

I finally got close enough to the top that I saw a patch of pink through the tree branches. "We're back."

"Are you okay?" The girl's voice was shaky, and I realized I'd almost forgotten about her.

"Yeah, he'll be all right." I didn't want to think about another outcome; it was just dawning on me that we'd been lucky he wasn't hurt worse.

Back at the trail, I lay Jack on the ATV and leaned over, hands on my knees, catching my breath.

Jack groaned. "Now what? Lucille's house is still a ways."

I stood back up. "We go on. She can ride behind me and you can sit in front."

"On your lap? No way!"

I held out my arms to the sides. "Do you see any other options?"

He glared. "No."

So I slid onto the seat, carefully arranging Jack so he sat sidesaddle on my lap, while the girl climbed on behind me and held tight. I remembered helmets then, but Jack's was in the chasm and mine was out of reach, not worth pushing Jack off and trying to get situated again. And I planned on going slow.

Jack held on to the handlebar with the hand of his good arm as I turned the key and we started moving. He shouted, "Again, you tell anyone about this and—"

I shouted back. "I'm dead to you! I get it."

He smiled a little, then cried out as I hit a bump.

"Sorry!"

Riding like that, we managed to keep going, slow but steady, and I breathed a huge sigh of relief when I finally saw Lucille's property. We pulled into the backyard just as the door to the house opened and Lucille came running out. She took one look at Jack and said, "I'll call 9-1-1."

"Wait!" Jack held out a hand to her. "Lucille, I just look really bad. Get me inside. We need to talk first."

I followed Lucille into the house with Jack in my arms. My clothes were filthy and I dripped water, but she didn't seem to care. I deposited him on a big flowered couch. She leaned toward him, her long gray hair covering most of her face as she looked him over. After a moment she straightened up, wiping her hands on her jeans. "You've got one minute, shorty, then I'm calling your father."

I mouthed *shorty?*

Jack waved me away and talked fast. "You know that guy this morning at the gas station asking about my truck? He's after her." He pointed behind me.

Lucille turned to look at the girl, who had just removed her helmet and stood there, her face flushed. Lucille looked her up and down, tapping the toe of her cowboy boot. "Is that true?" she asked.

The girl just sucked part of her bottom lip.

Lucille turned back to Jack. "Tell me what's going on."

"Get them some dry clothes first."

The girl ended up in a pair of Lucille's grandson's Levi's, which were only a little baggy. I was soaked through. For me, Lucille had to go up to the attic. "My dad was big, like you." She handed me a stack of clothes. "There might be something in here."

Without thinking, I asked, "What's that smell?"

"Mothballs." She smiled. "And they worked, too. You can't even tell these have been up there for twenty years."

The clothes were like something out of a vintage garage sale. I found an old flannel shirt that was soft and warm, and put it on over my T-shirt. Lucille's dad must have been huge, because the black pants I put on were almost loose. I was no fashion statement, unless the Paul Bunyan look was in.

After Lucille called Jack's father, Jack and I managed to get the whole story out while the girl paged through a section of the *Oregonian*.

As soon as we finished, Lucille walked into the kitchen, and I heard pots and pans start to bang.

I made a face at Jack.

He shrugged. "She thinks food solves everything."

The girl had been rustling through the paper, but the sound suddenly stopped.

I turned to where she sat, frozen, staring at the paper.

"What's wrong?"

She shook her head slightly. "I don't know. There's just something familiar."

"About what?" Jack asked.

She folded back the page and handed it to me.

My mouth dropped as I saw the section marked Literary Events, a picture of the scientist I'd seen on TV back at the cabin. Pointing, I said, "I just saw her on television. Dr. Kelly Emerson." I looked at the girl. "Do you know her?"

But then she frowned. "I don't think so. But . . . she just seemed familiar to me."

Glancing back at the page, I realized it was a notice for Dr. Emerson's book reading. "She's in Portland this afternoon."

Jack looked at me and raised his eyebrows.

"No." I shook my head. "I think we should just stay here, figure this out."

Jack said, "You could call your mom."

I nodded. She had to know more about this girl than I did. But I didn't know what, if anything, she would tell me.

The phone in the kitchen rang. Lucille answered, and then we heard a crash.

I jumped up and ran in there. Lucille was kneeling, picking up a pan of half-cooked eggs. Her eyes were wide when she looked up at me. "You and the girl need to go."

"Why? What happened?"

"There are more strangers at Jack's place; my son just drove past there. He said they were . . ."

"What?"

She stood up. "Combing. He said they were combing the area."

"For us?"

She lifted and lowered one shoulder as she set down the pan and picked up the phone.

Back in the other room, I said, "Jack, they're looking for us."

"Who?"

The girl stared at me as I shrugged. "I don't know. I can only think it has to do with . . ." My words trailed off as I looked at her.

Lucille stepped into the room. "Jack, your dad is meeting us at the hospital in Vancouver." Lucille handed me a set of keys. "To the Dodge truck out back. It's old, but it works."

Where was I supposed to go? I said, "If everyone is looking for her, shouldn't we just stay here?"

The girl spoke up. "They already found me once. We're too close here. They'll find me again."

Jack stabbed the newspaper with a finger. "Go to the book thing. See what you can find out."

I glanced at the photo of Dr. Emerson. "What makes you think she'll tell us anything?"

Jack looked at the girl and back to me. "It's either that or go back to Melby Falls and find your mom."

The girl stiffened at the mention of going back, so I knew that wasn't an option. Chasing down a former TroDyn scientist made no sense to me either. I just didn't see what was wrong with staying at Lucille's. For a while, anyway.

And I said as much. "We'll stay here for now, make sure you and Lucille get off okay."

The girl shook her head. "We can't stay here."

"Just for a while. It'll be okay."

She didn't respond, but her forehead wrinkled as she turned and stared out the window.

Lucille gathered her things while I carried Jack to her SUV and helped him spread out in the backseat. "Let me know you're okay."

"I'm gonna be fine." He patted his sling. "You be safe. And you know what I said before? Well, I'm kinda glad you were the hero. Thanks." He pulled on my shirt and I leaned closer.

He whispered, "Be careful. This may be one time when you don't need to be the hero."

I started to stand back up, but he pulled me down. "I'm serious, man. Just take it as far as you have to. You don't always have to see it through to the end. This girl is in something really frickin' weird."

That was the understatement of the century.

Jack shook his head. "You get the chance to hand her off to someone, just do it."

I nodded, even though I was certain I'd do just the opposite.

Back inside, Lucille reached up to the top of the fridge and pulled down a coffee can. She extracted a couple of twenties and handed them to me.

"I can't."

Lucille nodded. "Yes, you can. Shorty will pay me back." She jabbed a thumb toward the front door. She smiled. "You stay here as long as you need to."

I watched out the window as the SUV disappeared into the trees down the driveway.

"Mason!"

It was the first time the girl had called me by name, and it made me pause.

She called me again, louder, and I found her curled up on the couch, clutching a blue throw pillow to her stomach. Her eyes were wide. "They're coming."

EIGHT

"Now? How close are they?" I hoped we hadn't lost our window to get out of there, and I was already kicking myself for hesitating so long.

She stood. "We have a few minutes. Hurry."

Out in the garage, the girl and I climbed into the light green Dodge. The engine rumbled, like it was old and tired, and the shocks were nonexistent as I drove as fast as I could out the driveway. I hit a bump and my head smacked the ceiling.

At the road, I turned to go left, take the shortcut to hit the highway and go east, away from Jack's place, away from Melby Falls. But the shortcut road had deep muddy ruts, and the truck was too old to have four-wheel drive. We'd end up sitting ducks.

As I turned to go right, the girl pointed toward the shortcut. "We need to go that way."

"We can't."

I gunned the engine and we headed west. She tried to crawl into the space under the dashboard.

"What's wrong?"

And then I looked in front of me. Several vehicles were parked on either side of the blacktop road, and people in yellow slickers dotted the woods. "Stay down," I said, as I speeded up slightly.

As I passed the cars, a black one to my left looked familiar. In the backseat were the kids from the Haven, all three turning to look at the truck as I drove by, one meeting my gaze. The girl stayed hidden. But I doubted she could hide her mind, if that was what they saw. Or felt.

My hands started to shake as I forced myself to not tromp on the gas. I watched in the rearview mirror until we rounded a corner, then stepped on it. I needed to get away, fast, and going south made the most sense, so I drove toward the Bridge of the Gods to hit I-84.

The rain showed no signs of letting up, and actually turned into a downpour at times. Although I drove carefully, the slick curves in the road freaked me out.

I pulled on the girl's arm. "It's okay. You can get up now."

Slowly, she got back up on the bench seat. "They knew I was there."

"Did they tell anyone?"

"I don't know."

I sighed. "We have a little head start, I think."

But as I neared the on-ramp, I saw a police car with flashing lights and a line of cars. Turning into a gas station just before the line started, I left the engine running and told the girl to stay put.

The lady at the counter was jabbering with news, so I just listened. "A big rig jackknifed and hit a cattle truck. The semi is blocking both eastbound lanes and they're trying to move dead cows and find the ones that ran away."

A guy asked, "Any idea when it'll open back up?"

The lady shook her head.

Outside, I stood under the awning for a bit, watching the rain. East was no longer an option, not if I wanted to keep the distance between the girl and whoever those people in the woods were. I looked to my left. Maybe there were answers in Portland. Maybe this Dr. Emerson *would* know something, something that might jog the girl's memory. Even if she didn't, we couldn't sit there all day, waiting for the road to open up.

I turned the Dodge around and hopped on the westbound I-84.

The girl asked, "Where are we going?"

"Powell's." In Portland, the name Powell's meant only one thing: a bookstore. Not just any bookstore, but a bookstore that took up an entire city block. Sometimes my mom took me there on Saturday afternoons. Suddenly, it made sense to go to such a busy place. A busy place was better than an isolated cabin. I had to believe if someone was looking for us, the last place they'd look would be a bookstore.

The girl fell asleep with her head on the back of the seat. The girl. It was driving me crazy to keep referring to her that way, not knowing her name. I wanted to call her something, anything. But she hadn't suggested any such thing and it might be rude to just start calling her Blondie or whatever. It seemed like something that orderly at the Haven would have done. But did I really even want to know her name? Because if she remembered her name, then she'd remember where she belonged, and it might mean she'd go back to wherever she was from. That she'd go back to whatever life she had led before. And chances were, that life would not include me. Even though I'd known her less than twenty-four hours, I wanted to know her more. Even if that meant getting myself in more trouble.

As I drove, the gas gauge needle started dancing, then suddenly dropped from over a half tank to just above empty. "Oh, man." My mom had an old car once that did something similar; she never knew when the gauge was reliable or not. I did not want to take the chance of running out of gas halfway through Portland, possibly getting stranded on the side of the road, so I decided to head for the airport. We could take the light rail from there into the city.

Traffic was light as we turned north on 205. Once we got to the airport, I followed the signs to the short-term parking. I chose a parking spot far away from the terminal.

"Grab your coat."

She looked at me. "I didn't bring it."

As I frowned, she leaned back a little. I set a hand on her arm. "That's okay. It's a little warmer here than Glenwood." I didn't have a coat either.

"Are you hungry? We could get something on our way to the MAX?"

Inside the terminal I realized I was starving. The coffee and donuts of that morning seemed days removed. We went to the closest Coffee People kiosk, and I bought coffee and a muffin, then found a bench behind the door for international arrivals.

The girl didn't want anything to eat or drink. She people-watched, staring at one person until they were out of her sight, then picking another to study. She said, "The MAX is the light rail system in Portland."

Her statement sounded kind of like a recording. "How did you know that?"

"It came to me," she said, sounding more human. "Like it was there all along." A corner of her mouth turned up. "I just couldn't get to it at first."

Talk about confused. One minute it seemed she didn't know anything, the next it was as if she knew everything and just had to access it. I can't say the mystery made her less attractive.

She kept watching people walk by. "When does it leave?"

"They leave every fifteen minutes or so. It'll take about thirty minutes to get to the closest stop to the bookstore." I finished my muffin and brushed the crumbs off my hands. Walking past all the baggage carousels, it felt like we were travelers ourselves, just waiting to head on out into the world. At the end of the building, the MAX ticket machine sucked up my twenty, then pooped out two tickets and change.

We waited outside in a covered area. The rain had slowed to a steady drizzle. Not too many people were wait-ing for the train, but I couldn't help looking surreptitiously at the ones who were, wondering if anyone was following us, which was the tip of the iceberg as far as my worries were concerned. My mom knew Jack and I had gone to

Glenwood. And even if she did suspect we had the girl, would she have told anyone? Maybe she didn't have to. If the girl was important enough to have people following her, she probably had someone watching her. Someone besides my mom.

My eyes slowly drifted to the girl, who was running a finger up and down an advertisement for fresh produce. Could she be bugged somehow? She had said she was communicating with someone, and she had known someone was out front at the cabin before I even saw them through the scope.

Without thinking about it, I took a step back, away from her. Her eyes immediately met mine. "What's wrong?" she asked.

Her voice kind of shot right through whatever suspicions I had about her, and I stepped back beside her, itching to put my arm around her, hold her hand, anything, just to feel closer to her. "How's your head?"

She looked at me. "It's fine."

It wasn't easy to figure out how to ask what I needed to know. "Still . . . empty?"

Pausing before she spoke, she finally said, "No, not so much."

I didn't want to alarm her, make her think we should be worried about being followed. I tried to sound casual. "So, can you hear them?"

Her forehead creased and she didn't answer at first. Then she said, "It's comfortable again."

Was it possible that whoever was behind her condition could hear everything she heard? And was that how they managed to find us at the cabin?

The train arrived and we went to the very back so that we could face forward and see all the other passengers, including anyone who got on. Someone had left a few sections of newspaper on the seat and I opened one, holding it up in front of us, so that we were seated anonymously behind it. We were in our own cozy little cubicle made of newsprint. Might have even been romantic in other circumstances.

The rocking of the train eventually lulled her to sleep, her chin dropping down to rest on her chest. After a while, I folded the paper. I needed to see what was going on around us and was grateful for the gazillion milligrams of caffeine coursing through my body, keeping me awake.

A guy got on, older than me, probably college age from the looks of it. He studied his video iPod and wore an Oregon Ducks hat.

The headline of the sports section I'd been holding jumped out at me. It was the day of the Civil War game, when the Ducks played the Oregon State Beavers, pretty much dividing the state for a few hours.

The guy had taken off his dripping coat and set it beside him. He took off the Ducks hat, shook it, then set it back on his head. He had a big bag looped over one arm, which he kept the other arm securely around, and it covered the orange-and-black beaver on his sweatshirt. I smiled. Who would be stupid enough to wear both colleges' attire at the same time on the day of the Civil War game?

Then I froze.

No one, and I mean no one with half a brain, would be that stupid.

NINE

WITH A SIDEWAYS GLANCE, I COULD SEE THE GIRL WAS STILL asleep.

That guy in the conflicting sports getup could have sat anywhere on the train, but he chose a place near us. Not so near as to be obvious, but near enough to keep an eye on us. But he hadn't once looked our way. Had he? His eyes were glued to his iPod. I looked more closely at his bag. Particularly at a small tear near the seam. After rubbing my weary eyes, I looked again, trying to focus more on that hole. Could he have a hidden camera and be watching us that way?

Talk about paranoid.

Still.

Opening up the newspaper, I used it to hide us from the rest of the car again. I had an idea. We were getting off.

I woke the girl.

She asked, "Are we there?"

"Kind of." I got her to stand in front of me as we headed toward the doors. The guy stood up. He was closer to the door than we were. The guy was on my left, the girl on my right. I didn't dare look at him, but it was pretty obvious I had the size and weight advantage.

Gradually slowing, the train came to a stop. When the

doors opened, I held the girl back. The guy hesitated. The chimes sounded, signaling the doors were going to close, and in a flash, I whirled, grabbed the iPod, and shoved the guy out the doors just as they closed. As the train started to move, he glared at me and reached into his bag, yelling into a phone before we had gone fifty yards.

My hands were trembling as I peered at the iPod's screen. A song was playing. Some pop-star girl. I flipped through everything. Other than a few lousy movies and more girl songs, there was nothing to suggest anything amiss. "Oops. Guess I was a little paranoid."

The girl placed a hand on my shoulder. "You think he was watching me."

"They found you once. They can find you again." We took our seats. Great. I was just trying to help a girl and I stole some poor college kid's iPod. I turned around to look at the map and see how many stops we had left. If we stayed on the train for long, we might get hassled for stealing the iPod if the guy had called the cops. "We could get off at the next stop. It would just mean a longer walk."

She smiled. "That's fine. I like to walk." She sucked on her lower lip for a second. "I mean, so far, the walking we've done? I liked it. I'm not sure if I liked walking before."

A few minutes later, the automated voice announced the next stop and the train slowed.

I stood up. "Let's go." The doors opened. Dropping the iPod where the guy had sat, I held out my hand and the girl reached out and took it, and I had a feeling that was beginning to seem very familiar.

The drizzle was just enough to annoy and soak anyone out walking. With one arm, I held a section of the newspaper over our heads, while the other lay around her shoulders. We tried to stay under the awnings, but there weren't that many. Kind of stupid, in my opinion, given Portland is probably one of the rainiest cities in the country. Awnings should be mandatory. We'd gone about ten blocks when I felt her shiver under my arm. With the newspaper, I pointed at a Starbucks, then led her down a set of steps into the café, which was connected to an old hotel that looked new on the inside. A big fireplace sat in one corner. I motioned to a couch in front of it and told the girl, "You can sit here and get warmed up."

I shoved my wet newspaper into the garbage, then went to order coffee. The barista had a thick, silver ring, bull-like through his nostrils, a green streak in his purple hair. He didn't give me more than a token glance. I imagine he knew what it was like to be stared at.

The girl took the coffee and held it. We sat there in front of the fire, warming up and drying off.

The girl asked, "How much farther?"

"Not far at all." I jabbed my thumb to the right. "Just two blocks down there." I looked up as a couple walked in, but they were too busy looking at their kid in a stroller to notice us.

Was I crazy, looking for bad guys? What would the guy at the cabin have done if we'd let him in? Steal the girl?

She sat near the blazing fire, but still shivered.

"You okay?"

She nodded. "Just chilly. A little."

I took off my flannel shirt and gave it to her, though I kind of shivered in my T-shirt. So far, I'd let her be. Maybe it was high time to push it a little bit.

I thought about the story she'd told me, about the place where she sat, where the gardener came. "Can you tell me more about those visions you were having?"

She nodded. "They're more like memories, only kind of foggy. Like, when they are in my head, I feel a little removed. I'm not actually sure it was an experience or just something I dreamed up."

"When you remember the place, do you feel . . . ?" I wasn't sure how to ask what I wanted, so I came right out with it. "Were you a prisoner?"

She shook her head. "I don't think so. When I'm upset, I feel it here." She touched her stomach. "But I don't get upset when I have these memories. I don't really feel anything."

"Is it possible they didn't happen?" I asked, trying to keep my tone gentle. The story she'd told me at the cabin about being in a place before the Haven was just too odd. I had to face the idea that she might really have a brain injury, like my mom had said.

She looked at me for a moment. "Maybe. But if that's true, why am I like this? Walking around in a fog, not knowing who I am?"

I had no answer for her.

Holding the coffee between her hands, she lifted the warm cup to her face and held it there for a moment. "I'm not dumb."

I touched her arm. "I never said you were."

She didn't say anything, so I added, "I never even thought it."

The girl lowered the coffee. "I'm just a little out of sorts. Lacking common sense maybe, not sure how to deal with the everyday stuff. But trust me." She tapped her head and smiled a bit. "I've got a good brain in here."

I smiled back. "I'm sure you do."

We stayed there about fifteen minutes, but she didn't drink the coffee, just held it.

I said, "This seems to be some kind of pattern with you."

Her forehead wrinkled. "What?"

I pointed at her cup. "Beverage holding."

And, for the first time, she laughed, this wonderful giggle that made me chuckle along.

She stopped giggling but didn't stop smiling for a few seconds. But she still didn't drink any coffee.

I asked, "Aren't you hungry?"

She shook her head and held out the cup. "There's a little left."

I didn't want any more coffee, so I tossed both our cups into the garbage. Heading out, I grabbed a free arts newspaper from the rack near the door. "Umbrella." I held it over the girl's head as we stepped back into the drizzle.

We reached the street across from Powell's and weren't too drenched when we finally walked in the front door of the massive bookstore.

Inside, I grabbed a color-coded map from the stack on the counter. "This place is huge," I explained.

With four floors, numerous sections, and even a coffee-house, Powell's Books was an event. The girl stood, staring.

"What's wrong?"

"Nothing." Quickly she turned to me, the biggest smile I'd seen yet on her face, enough to make little wrinkles appear by the corners of her eyes. "Look at all the books."

Smiling back, I squeezed her hand.

She said, "I know it sounds funny, not knowing anything about myself. But I can tell, just from the feeling I have right now, that I love books."

My breath caught. As much as she was a stranger to me, I was starting to feel I knew her. But it wasn't enough. I wanted to know everything about her.

We walked over to the information desk, where a man in a ponytail and horn-rim glasses stood behind the wooden counter. His T-shirt said WILL WRITE FOR FOOD. His gaze rested appraisingly on the girl for a moment, then he turned to me, his eyes widening a bit before they locked with mine, avoiding my scar. I could almost hear him thinking *What is she doing with him?* Then he asked if he could help us.

I nodded. "Where's the Dr. Emerson talk?"

"You guys have a big interest in the food crisis?"

"Huh?" I glanced sideways at the girl.

The guy rubbed his beard a little. "The food crisis that Dr. Emerson's new book is about?"

Thinking fast, I said, "No interest other than a little extra credit."

"Aha. Gotcha." He pointed up. "Pearl, upstairs."

The sections of Powell's bookstore were color coded, purple, rose, gold, and so forth. But I thought it might be wise to browse in the stacks near the stairs for a bit. For what, I wasn't really sure.

The girl pulled out book after book, running her hands over the covers, then putting them back. She saw me watching her and blushed. "I can't help it. I want to touch them all."

As we looked at books, several people went up. No one seemed interested in anything other than heading up the stairs. Maybe I *was* being overly paranoid.

Finally, I looked at the girl and said, "Ready?" We climbed three flights to the pearl section. Like the rest of the store, it was a huge room in sections with rows and rows of bookshelves, stacked with hundreds and hundreds of books everywhere you looked. Several dozen metal folding chairs faced a screen and podium, where a lady in a blue dress fiddled with the microphone. She looked up at us. "Reading starts at three."

With the day we'd had, it already felt like midnight, but we were actually early. I led us over to a couple of couches. The girl dropped onto one with a sigh. She looked paler than she had before, which worried me. "You okay?"

With two fingers, she pinched the bridge of her nose and shut her eyes. "I don't know. I just feel kind of tired." Shaking her head slightly, she dropped her hand and blinked. Then she wrapped her arms around herself and shivered.

I reached out a hand and set it on her arm. "Still cold?"

Her expression went slack and she froze, seeming to ignore me. Then she spoke in a quiet, detached voice, as if she were telling me what someone else was experiencing.

"The arrival of the Gardener was met first with the trembling, then with a shared stirring, as if we were all awakening at once. We knew the arrival meant the stimulating part of our existence was about to occur.

"The Gardener moved to the front; the odd accompanying squeaks were familiar sounds to me. In anticipation, my heart beat faster. I waited for what I needed. Craved. Desired. And then, with a loud clank, the Gardener pulled the switch up front, and the light came."

God, it was so weird, like she was watching a movie, narrating it. I glanced around to see if anyone noticed. A woman and a little kid were looking at books nearby, but they weren't paying any attention to us.

"As one, our heads turned upward to the false sun. A murmur rose, like one big satisfying Ahhhhhhh. . . ."

The sound was too loud, and I quickly covered her mouth. She stopped. When I removed my hand, she spoke again.

"Revived vitality and strength seeped into me. Into us. I felt myself renewing, growing stronger, and I felt the shared strength emanating from my neighbors. My eyes opened and lowered as a small whirring sound preceded the opening of the small hole in the floor in front of me, from which rose a monitor, the same as the one that sat in front of the group. The screen flickered in blue, and I readied myself for that day's education."

She stopped speaking.

"What education?" I waved my hand in front of her face.

She finally met my gaze, but her hands were twisting together in her lap. "What?"

Hesitating just a little, I set a hand on hers. They were icy. "You said something about education. And I wondered, what education?"

Her gaze darted quickly from side to side. "I don't know. I'm remembering more. But it's just small . . . pieces. The books . . ."

"You remember books?"

She shook her head. "Not books. Information. There was a screen with information. So much."

"A computer? Is that the education?"

She hesitated, and then said, "Maybe." She sounded unconvinced.

Holding my breath, I pulled her close to me. I let out my breath. "We'll figure this out."

At that moment, the little kid walked over by us. He had red hair that stuck up, and there was a Transformer on his blue sweatshirt. He looked at the girl and said, "Hi."

She looked at me, then back at the boy. "Hi."

Wanting him to go back to his mother, I told the kid, "You shouldn't talk to strangers."

He stared at my scar for a moment. "Did a stranger do that to you?"

I probably could have gotten rid of him by lying and saying yes, but instead I shook my head. "It was a dog. A dog I knew, actually."

The girl reached up and touched my face. "I'm sorry."

I shrugged.

The boy pointed up at the girl's exposed arm. "Is that a butterfly?"

She twisted her arm to give him a better view of her tattoo.

He said, "Hey, I've seen that one before."

"You have?" she asked.

He nodded. "Want to see?"

The girl and I both said, "Yes."

The boy disappeared around the corner, and I half hoped he wouldn't come back. But a couple of minutes later he returned, hoisting a coffee table book in both arms. He plunked it down on the table in front of us. The cover photo was of a blue butterfly. The boy tapped it. "See?"

Leaning forward, the girl compared her tattoo to the butterfly on the cover. The boy sighed. "Oh. It's not the same one."

The girl frowned and said, "That's okay." She opened the cover and started paging through the book. "There are lots of blue butterflies in here."

The boy brightened. "Maybe we can find it."

"Maybe." The girl smiled. "Let's look."

As they searched, stopping at each page to compare the photos to her tattoo, I started to pay attention. Both she and my father had blue butterfly tattoos. But the video of my father was old and not that crisp, so it was hard to tell just how alike, or different, they actually were.

The boy squealed. "That's it! That's the one."

Taking a good look at both the book and her tattoo, I said, "Yeah, looks like it."

The boy's mom called him then, and he waved at the girl before running off. The girl was already leaning down to read the book, and I joined her. According to the book, the butterfly was the Karner Blue, about one inch across. I kept reading. The Karner Blue was completely dependent on one plant, the wild lupine, which they laid their eggs on. But with lupine becoming more and more scarce because of developers digging up and building on native prairie, the butterfly was losing its habitat.

"Bummer," I muttered.

The girl asked, "Are they endangered?"

I nodded, reading a bit more. "Yeah. They're pretty much toast. They probably should have expanded to different kinds of plants."

People started arriving and, before the seats filled up, we took seats near the back. The lady in the blue dress introduced Dr. Emerson's new book *When the Food Runs Out.*

Not exactly a picker upper.

The author was short, with dark hair to her shoulders, and wore a black suit with a white shirt. She immediately started referring to her PowerPoint, where a photo of Earth seen from space filled the screen. "Today in the world, approximately 120,000 people will die. Also today, approximately 360,000 people will be born. Meaning that, on the average, every two days we add the equivalent of the population of Portland to an already overcrowded world. But that doesn't affect you, right? That's what you're thinking?"

Actually, that *was* what I was thinking. I mean, I knew about overpopulation. But in Melby Falls, it wasn't high on my list of concerns.

"As long as you can drive your Hummer to Safeway and buy your groceries, this means nothing for you, am I right?"

Several people in the audience chuckled a bit, nodding.

The picture changed to a black-and-white portrait of an older guy in a white high-collared shirt. The author pointed. "Thomas Malthus, an economist born in 1766. His *Principle of Population* states that, first, food is necessary to the existence of man. Anyone disagree with that?"

Again, some chuckles. Most everyone shrugged and shook their heads.

She continued. "Second, passion between the sexes will always be there." She stopped and smiled. "To put it in simple terms for my younger audience members, people are not going to stop having babies."

Some people laughed.

The picture on the screen changed to a barren field with one cornstalk. "The problem is, as Malthus states, the power of population is greater than the power of the earth to provide enough food for that population."

A guy raised his hand, and Dr. Emerson pointed at him. He asked, "You're saying that, as the population grows, eventually we'll run out of food?"

Dr. Emerson nodded. "Yes, the Malthusian catastrophe— our return to subsistence-level conditions because population outgrows agricultural production."

The guy scratched his chin. "But isn't that unrealistic in this day and age, with all our technology? We're so far beyond subsistence. We have plenty of food and we keep coming up with better ways to grow food. I can see it being an issue in his day, but not in this century."

"Aha!" She pointed at the man. "A technological optimist. You believe that humans will always get out of every situation we get ourselves into."

The guy nodded and crossed his arms.

In front, the screen changed again, now to a map of Cuba. Dr. Emerson said, "Sorry to say, but this has happened, and quite recently. For decades, most of the food in Cuba came from Eastern Europe or was grown on big state-run farms with equipment provided by the Eastern Bloc countries. In 1989, the average Cuban was eating three thousand calories a day."

The picture changed to one of the Berlin Wall.

"But when the Eastern Bloc countries fell, Cuba's food supply was cut off, and their big farm operations were dependent on pesticides and on fuel for their machinery, which they no longer could get. Four years later, the average Cuban was getting only nineteen hundred calories a day, which is roughly equivalent to skipping one meal a day, and had lost twenty to thirty pounds."

A woman called out, "What did they do?"

Dr. Emerson raised a palm. "What could they do? They learned to grow food again, without relying on machinery or oil or pesticides to do it. The old-fashioned way succeeded. They are now back up to that average three thousand calories a day. And Cuba is a working model of sustainable agriculture. They don't rely heavily on machinery or fossil fuels or fertilizers. They can maintain what they are doing indefinitely."

Another woman raised her hand. "Are you saying we should all grow a garden?"

"In so many words." Dr. Emerson laughed a little, and then looked serious. "Here's the thing. Climate change, wars, and our dependence on oil: These all affect the food supply. And the day is coming when, as Malthus predicted almost two hundred years ago, the population will outgrow the food supply, and those of us growing vegetables in our backyards are going to deal with it much better than the people driving to Safeway in their Hummers. Because the day will come when even the grocery stores will be empty."

Next to me, the girl started to nod off and her head came to rest on my shoulder as I felt her deep, slow breaths. When Dr. Emerson finished and called for questions, hands went up. They were fairly dull and academic until the guy sitting in front of me raised his hand.

"Did you work on the food crisis when you were at TroDyn?"

Exactly what I was hoping for.

Dr. Emerson didn't miss a beat as she started to recite that well-rehearsed spiel, same as she had at the press conference, and the same as Jack had read to me at the cabin. "While my time with TroDyn was enriching to my career . . ."

I sat up straighter, accidentally waking the girl. She bolted up, startled.

Dr. Emerson glanced our way and faltered, her words trailing off as her eyes widened and one hand sprang to her parted lips.

I rolled my eyes. I mean, sometimes I forgot how strangers reacted to my face. Although that was the first time it had ever interrupted a lecture.

But then I realized she wasn't looking at me. The look on Dr. Emerson's face was clear and obvious, and could mean only one thing.

Dr. Emerson had seen the girl before.

TEN

DR. EMERSON SEEMED TO GET AHOLD OF HERSELF, BECAUSE after she finished her sentence, she quickly turned to the lady in blue and said something. Then the lady turned to the audience and said, "I'd like to thank you all for coming. That will conclude our program. The author will autograph your books at the front."

The girl shifted in her chair and I turned her way. "Did you see the way she looked at you? It was almost like..." My hand covered my mouth. Was it possible? It made sense. Why else would the author have been so stunned? "It was like she recognized you."

She didn't answer.

I noticed the girl seemed to be weaker. She just seemed *less* than she was before we got to Powell's. "Are you okay?"

She turned sideways in the chair and put her arm on the back, then lay her head down on it. "If I could just sit here for a little bit."

"Yeah." I looked up toward the front where people lined up with their books to get signed. That look on Dr. Emerson's face was just too odd to not investigate further. "We're gonna hang out and see if we can get a moment alone with the author."

The line showed no signs of shortening anytime soon, so the girl and I went over to the couch by the butterfly book.

When the last book had been signed, Dr. Emerson gathered her things. She stood and looked around for a moment.

Was she looking for the girl?

I stood up.

She noticed me, then her gaze dropped to the girl. Dr. Emerson quickly shook hands with the lady in blue, glanced our way once more, then walked around the corner to the stairs.

I debated. As much as I wanted to speak to her, ask her about the girl, she certainly didn't seem like she wanted to talk to us. Still, it was time to take a risk. "Come on." I grabbed the girl's hand.

We hurried down the stairs, just in time to see Dr. Emerson head into the second floor. We followed, turning the way she did, but she'd disappeared. A bright orange traffic cone sat in front of the men's room with a big CLOSED FOR CLEANING sign on it, and from inside, I heard the click of a mop on the floor. Hoping that Dr. Emerson was the only occupant of the ladies' room, I slid the cone over to block the entrance and pulled the girl inside.

The author stood at the sink, applying lipstick, and her hand froze midair as she saw us in the mirror. Her eyes locked on the girl. She turned around to face us. She fumbled with the lipstick, capping it and slipping it into the bag on her arm before moving toward us. "When I saw you in the audience, I . . ."

Not knowing exactly why, I stepped partly aside.

Her eyes narrowed as she moved closer to the girl, and her hands reached out.

The girl's eyes moved to me as she took a slight step back.

Dr. Emerson set a hand on either side of the girl's face. "It *is* you."

I grabbed her arm.

But Dr. Emerson shook me off as her eyes squeezed shut, tears spilling out. When she opened them, her eyes were glistening. "I never thought I'd see you again." Ignoring me, she pulled the girl to her chest in a deep hug and said one more thing.

"Laila. Beautiful Laila."

All I could do was stare as she continued to hold the girl and repeat her name. Part of me wanted to believe that it was just some trick. The other part wanted to believe that this mysterious girl would no longer be a mystery.

The girl peered at the author. "You know who I am?"

"Yes." Dr. Emerson turned to me. "Does she remember anything?"

I shook my head.

"What are you doing with her? How in the world did she end up here?"

Up to this point, I'd had too little sleep, too much caffeine, and no answers. I rubbed my eyes as I thought about what to tell her. When I dropped my hands, she had already turned back to the girl, who was frowning.

"I didn't know her name," I said.

"Her name is Laila." Dr. Emerson lifted the girl's chin with one hand, her eyes roaming all over. "You look pale. How are you feeling?"

The girl—it was hard for me to think of her as Laila—just shrugged a bit.

I was suddenly annoyed and impatient. Dr. Emerson seemed to know so much more than I did, and I wanted to know all of it. But first, I wanted to tell her something *she* didn't know.

"She practically threw me over a wall last night."

Once again, Dr. Emerson sized me up, scrutinizing my scar, her eyes widening a little at my size. "Did she really?"

I nodded.

Smiling, Dr. Emerson turned back to Laila and spoke very low, but I still heard her. "Thank God they didn't do it."

"Do what?"

She didn't answer me. She held the girl's . . . Laila's hand. "I don't know how you managed to get her here, but thank you. I'll take good care of her."

There was no way I was letting her take Laila. And I still wanted answers. Thrusting my chin upward, I asked, "Did you know her at TroDyn?"

She turned so fast I jumped. Her forehead creased as she asked, "Why would you ask that?"

Not sure about how much I wanted to reveal, not sure how much I could trust her, if at all, I said, "I didn't know anything about her. And she didn't know anything about where she came from or who she was. But something happened when she saw the lights of TroDyn."

Dr. Emerson stood up taller. "We did some medical work there. Case studies."

I said, "I thought TroDyn was all about sustainability."

Dr. Emerson's eyes narrowed. "They have research projects in many areas."

I muttered, "I'll bet they do." Still, I was surprised she'd say anything about TroDyn. I wondered if she'd say more, so I put some fake innocent cheer in my voice. "I'm applying for a summer program there."

She started to pull Laila toward the door.

"What are you doing?" I asked.

"Listen. What's your name?"

"Mason."

"Mason." Dr. Emerson spoke kindly for the first time since I'd met her. "I appreciate your escorting Laila here. You'll never know what it means to me to see her again. But you know and I know it's time for me to take over. My guess is that you're a nice guy, a nice guy who fell into this and, like Alice in the rabbit hole, have no idea what you're getting into."

Laila met my eyes and shook her head slightly. I could tell she still wasn't sure what to make of this woman. Not that she knew me, either, but I'd pretty much proved in the last twenty-four hours that she could trust me.

"We don't know you." I patted my chest. "All I know is *I'm* looking out for her. For Laila."

The corner of Dr. Emerson's mouth went up. "Look. I can see the attraction, damsel in distress and all that."

She really had no idea how little that helped her case.

She sighed. "I know you've known me for all of two minutes. But you have to trust me. I have Laila's best interests at heart and you are . . . you're a kid. You're not ready to follow this through."

Follow *what* through? Sticking with Laila until she got her memory back? Until she found her parents? "But I—"

She cut me off by leaning in close. She had coffee breath. "You have done a great thing. But this leads nowhere good for you. So it's time for you to just walk away." She waved her hand a little bit. "Walk away. Pretend you never met this girl."

Taking in Laila, her brown eyes, I knew I couldn't do it. "No. I'm not going anywhere."

Laila clutched my hand even tighter.

Dr. Emerson frowned. "You do know you'll run out of options. You'll have to let me take her . . . eventually."

I asked, "Take her where?"

She sighed. "Haven't you figured it out? I want to get her where they can't get their hands on her anymore."

I asked, "Who do you mean by they?"

She looked at me like I was something to scrape off her shoe. "You already know who they are."

Had to be TroDyn.

"I'm not ready to hand her over yet. Not before you tell us everything." Even then, there was no way I was going to abandon Laila, but Dr. Emerson didn't need to know that. Yet.

"I'll go along with your little mission or whatever," Dr. Emerson said. She smiled at Laila. "You're going to be fine."

Laila's forehead wrinkled as she looked up at Dr. Emerson. "I'm remembering things. Just starting to. I was in this place."

Dr. Emerson leaned closer to Laila. "What do you remember?"

Laila looked at me first, then back to her. "A place. There were others, and . . ." Her eyes went blank again, like before, and I wondered what she was remembering. And then she started to speak in that same detached voice.

"The monitor and the light. The monitor and the light. That's all there is. Until . . ."

She paused for a moment, frowning. Then she continued, "Until that day, the day the Gardener was not alone. Footsteps, many footsteps . . . They invaded our place. I wasn't afraid, just curious. Why were others with the Gardener? But the Gardener's voice was different that day. I felt a ripple of something make its way toward me. Something I'd never felt before. Something . . ."

Dr. Emerson looked puzzled as Laila started to tremble and her breaths became quicker, shorter. Her voice changed, became a whimper. "It started. The shrieks from the end of the row that turned into screams that gradually came closer one by one. It was my turn. And then, I didn't know them before, fear and pain. But they rolled into one new giant feeling as, for the first time, I felt . . ."

"What?" I asked. "What did you feel?"

Laila looked at me, her eyes wide, and she screamed as she extended an arm toward me. But just as I reached out, her eyes rolled back in her head and she slumped over. I caught her before she fell.

Her head lolled as her eyes fluttered.

Just then, a man hurried in, wearing blue overalls and pushing a yellow plastic mop bucket on wheels. "I heard a scream."

Scooping Laila up, I brushed past him and the startled expression on his face. In the empty hallway, I hesitated.

Dr. Emerson was right behind me. "What do you think you're doing?"

"We've got to get her out of here." I stopped and turned around. "She needs help."

"You have no idea what's wrong with her."

She was right. I had no idea. But I knew what I had seen so far. "She's been getting weaker ever since we left Haven of Peace. I mean, that was when she seemed the strongest. It's like she's gone downhill since then."

Dr. Emerson said, "Tell me about her there."

The vision of those four sitting on the couch, looking eerie and sedated, was pretty easy to call up. "Well, they just sat—"

She frowned and held up a hand. "Back up. *They?*"

I nodded. "Yeah, there were four kids, all sitting together on the couch. . . ." Although I didn't want to tell her everything I knew, the story of what had happened at the nursing home flowed out before I could stop.

After I was done, Dr. Emerson's brow wrinkled as she held a hand to her lips and cocked her head.

"What?"

She stared at Laila a few seconds more, and then shook her head slightly as she dropped her hand. "I have a car downstairs."

My options seemed pretty limited. I could try to get Laila some medical help, but they would ask so many questions, questions I had no idea how to answer. Dr. Emerson had distanced herself from TroDyn for a reason. Maybe, for Laila's sake, I could take a chance and trust her.

When Laila came to in the elevator, she was still weak. With an arm around her waist, I held her up as we rode down to the parking garage and followed Dr. Emerson to a blue Prius with rental stickers.

After we'd buckled in, I said, "Tell me what you know."

She shook her head. "I'm not the best city driver, so just wait until we get there."

I tried asking her questions, but she held me off, saying she needed to concentrate. After what had happened that morning on the ATV, I was willing to give her the benefit of the doubt.

Dr. Emerson constantly fidgeted while she drove, reaching up to scratch her cheek or run her fingers through her hair. I was nervous, too, but tried not to show it. At the Hilton, we took the elevator up to her suite and I helped Laila over to a white couch, where she curled up and closed her eyes. I dropped to the floor and leaned back against the couch.

My stomach rumbled.

"You're hungry." Dr. Emerson stepped over to the desk and tossed me a thick, white book. "Call room service. We may be here for a while."

I was starved, but I set the book aside. "Just tell me what is going on."

Dr. Emerson walked over to the mini bar, broke the seal, and pulled out a bottle of Pellegrino. "Want anything?"

I shook my head.

After pouring herself a glass, she came back and sat on a chair across from me. "I'm telling you, again, to just walk away. If you know what's best for you."

Laila might have been asleep already, but I lowered my voice in case she wasn't. "I don't care about what's best for me right now. I care about her."

Dr. Emerson raised her glass to me. "Noble. Very noble, Mason." She took a drink. "But you don't even know this girl." She leaned forward, obviously intending for Laila not to hear what she was saying. "Believe me, she has issues you couldn't even imagine. Are you really willing to put your entire world on the line for her? Because that's what you're doing if you stay here."

I crossed my arms. "Spill. Everything. I want to know."

Laila coughed a little, then propped herself up on an arm and looked at us. "You're talking about me."

When neither of us said anything, she said, "I want to know. If this is about me, it's only right."

Dr. Emerson set her glass down and ran both hands through her hair. "Laila, you had an accident resulting in head injuries. Your parents chose to put you in an experimental recovery program run by TroDyn. Nothing more."

That made no sense. "Then why do you want to keep her from them? The people at TroDyn?"

She hesitated slightly. "I didn't agree with some of the . . . procedures. And I found myself at odds with the director of the program. I'd rather see Laila get help somewhere else."

"But don't you need her parents' permission to take her out of the program?"

Again, a small pause. "They'd given up, all the parents. Unless their children came back completely whole, they felt it best to leave them with TroDyn."

Laila's eyes welled up, but I didn't believe Dr. Emerson for a second. Parents wouldn't just give up on their children, no matter how injured they were. She was lying about some, if not all, of it. There had to be more. "Why would they come looking for her in Glenwood?"

Dr. Emerson shrugged. "I'm sure it wouldn't look good for them to lose her. Think about it. A girl with amnesia turns up, the only thing she knows for sure is she is afraid of TroDyn? The media would catch on, putting TroDyn in a very difficult situation. The parents might pull the kids out of the program. . . ." She trailed off.

Her words sounded hollow. I just didn't believe the past twenty-four hours could all be attributed to a lost test subject.

I had to get Dr. Emerson to tell me the truth.

Getting to my feet, I turned toward Laila as I said, "So I might as well take her back."

Dr. Emerson's response was immediate. "You can't!"

"Why not?" asked Laila.

I whirled around. "Yeah, why not? She's just a test subject, right?"

Dr. Emerson was on the edge of the chair, her eyes wide. "Right. But—"

I waited.

A big sigh came out as she leaned back. "Wrong. That's not it at all."

"Then tell us. Tell us how you know her. Tell us what TroDyn is doing."

She didn't say anything, and I moved to pick up Laila.

"No, wait. Just . . . just leave her, okay? I'll tell you." Dr. Emerson stood up and began to pace. "I was just through with my PhD in research biology when TroDyn hired me to work on species and sustainability. In my interview, management presented cutting-edge ideas on how to manage food crises around the globe, food shortages, droughts, even the impending problems global warming will cause. As I said in my lecture, the end of food is not far off. I wanted to do something about it, and TroDyn seemed a perfect fit for me."

Questions flew through my mind, but I forced myself to stick with basics, leave the tough ones for later. "What kind of project did you work on?"

Laila asked, "How did you know me?"

She sighed. "That's where it gets complicated. I'd been working with these nudibranchs, marine snails that had developed the ability—"

"To make their own food," I interrupted.

Dr. Emerson appeared startled that I knew.

I shrugged. "I like biology." I sat down on the floor in front of Laila, my back against the couch.

Dr. Emerson looked down a moment, gathering her thoughts. "I'd been working with the nudibranchs for a while when one of the scientists approached me about a new experiment related to the snails, but on a much more practical level that could be directly applied to the food crisis."

She paused in her pacing and sat down on the ottoman. "This is not going to sound good. And it may be hard for you both to hear. But you must understand I truly was passionate about finding an answer to starvation. I mean, to actually be able to count yourself as one of the scientists who solved a crisis like that? Especially when the future will see all of us struggling for food during climate change."

She was already making excuses, coming off as defensive. Why? Rubbing my eyes with both hands, I asked, "What did you do?"

She shook her head. "No. Don't take that attitude with me. This started long before I ever showed up at TroDyn. Long before."

I nodded. "Go on."

"They took me to see the scientist who'd been working on the autotroph project."

My eyes widened. "Autotrophs?"

Laila asked, "What's that?"

Dr. Emerson met my gaze. "Self-feeders, organisms that can produce their own food."

"You're talking about snails, right?"

Dr. Emerson took a long drink. Over the top of the glass, her eyes drifted to Laila.

I lowered my voice. "Tell me it was snails." I shut my eyes, and my final plea was only a whisper. "Please tell me it was snails."

Laila's hand grasped mine and squeezed.

Dr. Emerson said nothing.

I opened my eyes. "Tell me." My voice was nearly a shout, and she winced.

She said, "It wasn't snails. Mason, it wasn't snails we were turning into autotrophs." Her head fell into her hands. "God help me, it wasn't snails."

ELEVEN

I shouted, "What does that mean?"

Scrunching her eyes shut, her words all came in a rush. "Laila was part of the second phase of the autotrophs experiment, raised from the time she was a baby to develop the ability to self-feed. The scientists kept them in a room with artificial sunlight that they used to create nutrients. I didn't know about it until she was nearly ten. They'd already been doing it for a decade."

Laila gasped, and I dropped her hand. In a flash, I launched myself away from the couch, scrambling to get away from the girl, from Laila, whatever she was. Smacking my head on the corner of the nightstand, I ended up on the floor, smashed up against the bed. My heart pounded and I couldn't say anything.

Laila had covered her face with her hands and was rocking back and forth, saying something I couldn't hear. Then she curled up, facing away from me. Her breathing evened out until she seemed to be sleeping.

Dr. Emerson sat next to her, rubbing her back. "You don't have to be afraid of her. She hasn't changed, Mason. She is who she is."

But she wasn't . . . what I thought. Not just a girl. She was something else.

Words eked out. "How did that happen?"

Dr. Emerson swallowed. "As I said, it was the second phase. The first phase had . . . worked out a few kinks, and I came on board with the second phase." She started to sound more excited. "But with the second phase, we did it. These children actually were able to feed themselves—"

"Hold on," I interrupted. "Children?"

Dr. Emerson's mouth was a thin line.

My confusion and bewilderment were overruled as I glared at her. "Where did you get the children?"

She held both her hands up. "It's not what you think. They were all children of TroDyn employees, and their parents knew what they were doing. Those who didn't want to participate were given the chance to leave."

I thought back to what Jack had found on the Internet, the similarities between the ex–TroDyn employees, that they'd all had babies within months after leaving. Was that why? They didn't want their children to be part of the experiment?

Dr. Emerson spoke slowly now. Maybe she'd figured out I wasn't going to completely freak. "The ones who left weren't as committed, obviously. But the ones who stayed, they were deeply . . . passionate about finding a solution to world hunger. To them . . . to me, it was . . . *is* as real a challenge as curing cancer. Those scientists truly thought they could do it and it was worth enrolling their children in the project." She looked over at Laila. "And keeping them in it."

I leaned back on my haunches. "Why did you leave?"

"A disagreement in philosophies." She raised her chin, seeming to gain strength as she talked about her defection from TroDyn. "I agreed with the concept, giving humans the ability to make their own food, not having to rely on weather or other humans for nourishment. And I believed it could be done fairly simply, giving the subject a normal life in the process. This is what the project looked like to me when I came on board."

"The project?"

"It began when the children were babies. The head scientists weaned them from food nutrients and developed a process of garnering nutrients from the sun." Her voice was firm. "As long as the amount of sunshine was perfectly regulated, the child maintained a perfect balance of nutrients, requiring neither food nor water."

I didn't believe it. "That's it? Just sit the kid in the sun and they're an autotroph?"

"It would seem that way." A line appeared between her eyes. "I didn't know all the intricacies of the process. Each of us knew only parts of the full recipe, just enough for us each to do our jobs. Mine was to monitor the children." She rested a hand on Laila. "She was one of them. What I didn't know was that as the children got older, they couldn't maintain that perfect balance through adolescence. So TroDyn wanted to change the experiment. They wanted to add an artificial element to boost the anomaly. Artificial horizontal gene transfer."

My stomach turned. I got it. Unfortunately. "They're playing God."

Dr. Emerson came over and sat down on the chair, smoothing her skirt under her. "The evolution was not going to happen on its own." She paused, and when she spoke again, her voice took on that lecture tone. "There is a genus of lizard called Anolis that lives on a Caribbean island having varying geographic features. Scientists studying these lizards realized that even though the genus on the island was the same, the different habitats had caused them to develop different abilities.

"The species that lives near tree trunks in the rain forest developed longer legs for running and jumping quickly, while another, which lives on twigs in the rain forest, has short legs for maneuvering on the smaller surface. Over generations, more than 300 species developed, and they adapted to their specific environments. Evolution on a small scale."

I made a face. "But that doesn't just happen."

"You're right." Dr. Emerson shook her head slightly. "Changes happen at the genetic level, and individuals inherit those new characteristics that give them more of a chance to survive. Around the tree trunks, longer-legged lizards were more apt to survive, and then they reproduced, creating lizards with longer legs, until gradually the entire population had longer legs, perfectly suited for their habitat."

I said, "Natural selection. Survival of the fittest."

"Yes." She nodded. "Adapt or die."

I cleared my throat. "So is TroDyn attempting to adapt humans to a foodless planet?"

She nodded.

Amazing. "Because we couldn't adapt to something like starvation. We'd die from it first."

She said, "You're right. And if we look at the history of species evolution, like the lizards, it will take more than a few generations to develop the true autotroph. Which is why they wanted to employ an artificial element."

"Artificial?" Did I really want to know?

She explained, "A technological element combined with an organic one, to help regulate the self-feeding ability."

It seemed ridiculous: They were building eco-cyborgs? Impossible. "There's no way . . ."

"Exactly. It's purely theoretical. I mean, I saw sketches." She lowered her head. "Although they couldn't have seen it through, just the thought of it was . . ." She looked down at her hands, which were clasped in her lap.

"The thought of what?"

She sighed before meeting my gaze. "Basically, they give the subjects a root system, made up of half organic material and half technological device, an advanced chip, designed to mutate the genes on a cellular level while connecting each of the children to each other, forming an artificial symbiosis that works like the real thing."

"Wait." I made myself take a deep breath as what she said sank in. "They wanted to put computerized roots in them?"

Dr. Emerson tucked some hair behind her ear. "That's a layman's way of looking at it. The technology would work with the organic material to speed up the change in the genome, rewrite the structure of the gene, so that it could then be inherited by the very next generation."

I let my breath out. "Evolution. They wanted to force evolution." My hands were trembling and I sat on them. Her silence told me I was right. And I thought of Laila when she went into her trance, talking about that other place. Could it be true? Had she been remembering? "What did the kids do there?"

"They were educated, highly so. I'm sure they learned more than you ever learned in school."

There was no comprehending any of it. "But why educate them if they're just subjects in an experiment?"

Dr. Emerson sighed. "That's another place where I had issues. They weren't just part of the experiment. They were being groomed to work at TroDyn. Which I suppose I understood. It's not as if they could have worked on the outside, and TroDyn couldn't have hired new scientists at that phase of the experiment."

"Wait a second." It just seemed so ridiculous, all that going on in Melby Falls. "Then how can they bring in people for internships and jobs if they can't let anyone know what is going on?"

She smiled. "Believe me, TroDyn is so big you could work there for years and never guess the autotroph experiment was even happening. It was always the corporation's other pursuits that funded this experiment. They still do, which is why TroDyn is always in the news for its work with global warming, new technology to deal with oil spills and nuclear reactor incidents. And why they will always need more employees. Those employees just won't ever have access to a major part of the facilities."

"Why didn't you stay and work with one of those?"

She shook her head. "I couldn't stay there, knowing what I knew. I couldn't have stayed away from the kids, I guess. I had to leave."

I wondered what was supposed to happen when the kids grew up. "If it takes a few generations to adapt . . ."

She nodded. "This was another place I disagreed. Because in order to truly evolve, each Phase Group would have to mate among themselves to produce the next generation. Like the lizards with the longest legs mating to produce lizards with longer legs. And I thought that . . . well, it went beyond any scientific method I had ever heard of."

I felt as if I might be sick. "And experimenting on kids is so moral?"

She straightened up. "For the greater good, I say it was. Their parents had the right to decide for them."

I kicked the ottoman. "You make it sound like they were deciding whether or not to let them go on a date! Hello, they gave up their children!"

She folded her arms in front of her and shut her eyes. "It wasn't that simple at all. I know it sounds . . . strange." She opened her eyes. "But to be able to fix a universal problem that's only going to get worse? I mean, look at me. I travel the country trying to convince people to plant their own gardens and quit driving gas guzzlers. And we're too late for it to work. Changing our behaviors now is not going to save the planet. But the autotroph program was skipping a few steps; we were doing something that mattered. It was a sacrifice, but it was the needs of a few against the needs of the many. The needs of the many will always be more important." She held out her hands, palms up. "Don't they have to be?"

I stood up and walked over to the couch, then knelt in front of Laila. "What about her? What kind of life is it for her?"

Dr. Emerson dropped her hands and met my eyes. "That's exactly why I resigned. I saw where it was going. I didn't see how they would achieve the results they wanted while staying in moral boundaries that I could live with. And the . . ."

Her moral boundaries seemed a bit lax to me. But her trailing off made me intrigued. "And the what?"

She shook her head a bit. "Nothing."

"You can't stop now."

"It's just . . ." She scratched her cheek again, like in the car. "A faction of the scientists had higher aspirations. Financial pursuits."

I couldn't imagine Walmart offering autotrophs anytime in the near future.

She saw my puzzlement and explained. "The military would have paid big money. Can you imagine? Perfect soldiers that need neither food nor water."

I almost groaned. Hogan had called it that day in biology. "But they didn't do it?"

Dr. Emerson shook her head. "Still, it will always remain a possibility. Especially for one of the lead scientists, who was hell-bent on the idea. And I couldn't live with that. Monitoring those children just so they could grow up and be soldiers."

"And TroDyn just let you go? No problem?"

She smiled a little, as her eyes narrowed. "There's always a problem. No one just leaves TroDyn scot-free. Among . . . other things, I signed a confidentiality agreement. I agreed to never work for a competing company in the same area."

"That's it? No blood oath?"

She laughed. "No."

I asked, "Did you have a kid?"

She shook her head. "No." She looked for a long while at Laila. "They had become my children in some ways. Being with them all day. Teaching them, learning from them." She sighed again. "I couldn't bear to see what they were going to do to them in order to get the results they needed."

"So you walked out on the children?" I couldn't help myself.

Her eyes narrowed. "No, of course not. There was nothing I could do."

"Still, you pretty much bailed."

She looked down at the floor for a moment, and when she looked back up, her eyes were full of tears. She motioned toward Laila, but had trouble speaking at first. "These . . ." She swallowed. "These kids, like Laila? They were like my own. Leaving was the hardest thing I've ever done. But I couldn't stay there and watch. I couldn't."

I asked softly, "What did they have over you?"

"Them. The kids. Like Laila. They said if anyone tried to stop the experiment, there would be nothing to find."

"What would they do?"

"Whatever they had to."

I was confused. "But they couldn't hurt them. Wouldn't that ruin the experiment?"

She raised one shoulder and dropped it. "Is that a chance you'd be willing to take? Because I'm not. But I had resigned myself to never seeing any of them again. And now . . ."

"What about the people with kids? The ones who didn't want them in the experiment?"

"Same thing. Confidentiality agreement."

I shook my head. "How did they guarantee you didn't just go running around, telling the world?"

"The people expecting children knew what was at stake. Their children. They would never be safe if they didn't stick to the agreement. And there was the compensation, of course."

Compensation? "You mean, like a fund?"

She nodded. "Some employees were able to secure a monthly payment. It seemed like extortion to me, taking the money to keep their mouths shut. I didn't need it, but some of them expecting children probably did."

Yeah. I knew of one in particular.

"Did they think TroDyn would come after them if they talked?"

Dr. Emerson shrugged. "Again, who would be willing to take that chance?"

I saw her point. Laila was my age. What if our situations were reversed? What if our parents had made different choices?

How could our parents live with this knowledge and not do anything?

Dr. Emerson looked at Laila with true affection, even

I could see that. My voice was almost a whisper as I asked, "And you're sure they haven't done what you were saying? Added the technological part?"

"Yes." She frowned a little. "I mean, look at Laila. There's no . . ."

"No what?"

She bit her lip as she got to her feet and walked over to me. She asked, "Have you seen her use the bathroom this whole time?"

I blushed. "I don't know."

Dr. Emerson asked, "And did she drink anything?"

"Yoo-hoo." I shook my head. "No, actually . . . No, she didn't drink any of it."

"Did she eat anything?"

"She had donuts."

She gasped. "She did?"

I looked down at the floor. "But then she threw up."

In a strong, sudden movement, Dr. Emerson shoved me aside as she groped for Laila's arms, repeating "They couldn't, they couldn't, they couldn't" as she turned them over one at a time, squinting her eyes to scan every inch of them.

"What are you looking for?"

Laila moaned and woke up, pushing Dr. Emerson away as she pulled up Laila's shirt, peering at her back. "Stop it," Laila said, trying to scrunch herself into a corner of the couch.

"What are you looking for?" I asked again.

Dr. Emerson ignored me, continuing to analyze Laila's skin. "I'm afraid . . ."

That didn't sound great. I grabbed her arm, forcing her to stop what she was doing and look at me. "What? You're afraid of what?"

She ran her hair back with one hand and glanced at Laila. "That they may have actually done it."

Laila's voice was loud. "*What?* Done what?"

Dr. Emerson sank to the edge of the couch. "I'm not entirely sure, but there would probably be marks or scars."

Laila shook her head as she looked at me. "I don't have any scars." She held up her arms. "Look. Look for yourself."

"Yes, you do." My heart beat faster. "She has scars on the back of her legs."

Laila's mouth dropped open as she ran, stumbling on her weak legs, for the bathroom. She got the door shut and locked before either Dr. Emerson or I could grab her. With a flat hand, I pounded on the door. "Laila, open the door."

Nothing.

Dr. Emerson was beside me. "Laila, please. You have to let me in."

Silence.

"Please, Laila."

Laila's voice sounded small and scared. "If I have the scars, what will it mean?"

Dr. Emerson rested her forehead on the door and sighed. "Laila, just open the door and we can—"

"No!" Laila's shout made me jump. "You tell me! Tell me what it means!"

Dr. Emerson sighed. "It might mean . . ."

I asked, "What? It might mean what?"

The doctor just shook her head and went over to the couch, where she sat down and put her head in her hands.

A few moments passed with no sound from inside the bathroom. Then a long, anguished wail.

"Laila!" I pounded on the door. "Open up!"

The lock clicked and the door fell open. Laila's face was shiny with tears as she stood there in the doorway in her white underwear, her jeans around her ankles. "What does it mean?" She turned around, revealing the scars that began on the backs of her thighs and continued down to her calves.

Dr. Emerson gasped as she walked over to us.

Laila fell to her knees in front of Dr. Emerson, grabbing her skirt and burying her face in it. "Tell me."

Dr. Emerson leaned over, her hands holding Laila's face. "I'm so sorry, I'm so sorry." She looked over at me. "It's too late. They did it."

I didn't understand. "What? They did what?"

Dr. Emerson took in a big shuddering breath and said, "The Greenhouse. They rooted her."

TWELVE

SHE SAID IT AGAIN, WITH MORE DESPERATION IN HER VOICE. "They *rooted* her."

"You mean . . ." The experiment she'd talked about. The experiment that had been only theoretical, technology meshing with the organic and speeding the evolution. I stared at the scars on Laila's legs. Scars like that didn't come without pain and suffering. I knew firsthand about things like that. "Oh my god."

Laila collapsed.

Dr. Emerson was pale and her hands shook as she removed Laila's jeans. "Can you carry her to the bed?"

I lifted Laila, trying to ignore the fact I'd never been this close to a girl in her underwear, if Laila could in fact be considered a girl. Although holding her in my arms, she seemed like nothing *but* girl.

"Is she going to be okay?" I asked as I laid her down.

Dr. Emerson tucked the covers around her. "I'm not sure."

I glanced at her. "What are you talking about? She's just weak, we'll just take her to a hospital, get her some medicine or some rest. . . ."

"Don't you understand?" Dr. Emerson wiped tears off

146

her face with one hand. "A hospital can't help her. She drew her strength from the others. That was part of the next phase of the experiment, after the rooting, to get them out of the Greenhouse, see if their symbiosis was enough to keep their abilities without the constant sun and warmth. None of it would be valid if they had to just sit in the Greenhouse forever. The process had to have practical applications."

I sat down on the edge of the bed. "The Greenhouse?"

Dr. Emerson set a hand on my arm. "Without the others, she's lost her strength. She can't do it on her own. She can't give herself what she needs."

From where I sat, I could feel Laila's warmth. "There must be something we can do." Laila's eyelashes fluttered, and I wondered if she was dreaming. What would she dream of? Life in a greenhouse?

Maybe she dreamed of freedom.

Maybe she dreamed of me.

Dr. Emerson's voice was gentle. "Short of taking her back to TroDyn, no, there's nothing we can do."

"Then we have no choice." I turned. "We take her back."

She slammed her hand down on the night table. "Absolutely not. I won't allow it."

I pointed at her. "I don't think it's up to you."

She laughed. "Are you serious? Who put you in charge?"

"I'm the one who got her out of there. I'm the one who's taking care of her, and I'm going to keep taking care of her." I touched Laila's arm, then took hold and shook it a bit. "Hey. Wake up."

"She's had a shock." Dr. Emerson grabbed my arm, not unkindly. "Let her rest."

"She's better off alive than dead."

"Not always." Her eyes moved down my scar and back up.

"You've got to be kidding me. You think I'd be better off dead than look like this?"

"No, not for a second. But trust me: Her existence was not what you or I would call living."

"Still." My hand drifted to Laila's hair and I let it rest there a bit. She was so beautiful and peaceful. Whatever it meant for her, I couldn't live with myself if I let her go. I turned back to Dr. Emerson. "Will you tell me how to get her in?"

Her shoulders slumped. "Oh, they'll open the doors wide when you show up with her. I can only imagine the search they've put on."

I scratched my chin as it dawned on me that someone else would be freaking. Mom would be worried. But then, why hadn't she called? I pulled my phone out of my pants. I'd forgotten I had turned it off. There were eleven missed calls, all from my mom. I locked myself in the bathroom. She answered on the first ring. "Mason?"

"Yeah."

Her words were quick and quiet. "Where are you? Are you all right?"

"We're in Portland."

"You and Jack? Why aren't you at the cabin?"

I grimaced. She had no idea about anything that had happened in the less than twenty-four hours since we'd left the Haven. Unless she'd jumped to some conclusions. We did disappear at the same time as one of her charges. "We . . . had some stuff to do."

"Oh." She sounded weary.

"Mom? You okay?"

"I haven't been drinking, if that's what you mean."

"No, it's not that. You sound tired."

"I've been up all night. There's trouble at work."

"Mom . . . I need to tell you something." And I told her, everything that had happened up until Powell's. After that, I just couldn't go there. "Did you suspect? That Jack and I . . ."

"I wondered," she said. "They took the others. After they found out the girl was gone."

"Back to TroDyn?"

She inhaled sharply, and then said, "Yes."

"I know what they are. The kids."

She sighed.

"What's going on?"

"You need to come home. I'll tell you everything."

Everything? "Mom, are you taking money from TroDyn?"

Her answer was quiet. "Yes."

"Because of me."

"And I've put it all away for you." She was silent for a moment. "Mason, we can deal with this."

"The girl, she might be dying. How do we deal with that?"

She was silent. "I'm not sure there's anything you can do about that."

"There has to be. Someone at TroDyn will help her."

She whispered, "I don't want you there. Promise me."

"Then tell me where to go, Mom. Tell me where else to go to save her."

Her answer was immediate. "There is nowhere."

"Besides TroDyn, you mean."

"Do *not* go there."

"You can't stop me." I slapped my phone closed and unlocked the bathroom door.

"How long does she have?" I asked Dr. Emerson.

She laid a hand on Laila's cheek. "About as long as anyone would have without food or water. Probably less, since she'd been relying on symbiosis rather than direct feeding from the sun."

"Would sun help?"

She nodded, and then tilted her head toward the window, where the sky was still completely overcast. "Got any?"

"Could we take her to a tanning booth or something?"

"No. The lighting at TroDyn was a true replication of sunlight. Tanning beds have some rays filtered out. It would be like you drinking a glass of milk that had Vitamin D and calcium stripped from it. Nothing you can use. And the sun would be only a temporary fix anyway. Until she's an adult, she still requires the symbiosis."

A glimmer of hope planted itself in my gut. "What happens when she's an adult?"

She scratched her head. "Again, I'm just working off of theory, but the scientists thought that once the kids stopped growing, they might retain their abilities to photosynthesize without needing anyone else. They might be able to live in-dependently. Possibly. Again, it was just theory, not tested."

"Why didn't TroDyn just do it all in a sunny climate?"

"They needed to be in complete control, regulate the sun-light perfectly. To turn it on and off as they needed. Even Hawaii has cloudy days. And to be honest, TroDyn has a bottom line just like every other company. They got some tax breaks that wouldn't happen in Hawaii or California."

"So how long do we have?"

"Maybe twenty-four hours. All we can do is make sure she's comfortable."

To hell with that. I grabbed Laila's jeans off the couch and pulled back the covers.

Dr. Emerson frowned. "What are you doing?"

"Getting her dressed."

She asked, "Why?"

"I'm getting her some help." I picked up Laila's ankle and started dressing her.

"You can't!" Dr. Emerson grabbed my arm, and I shoved her off.

"I'm not going to sit here and watch her die when there is someone who can help her."

Dr. Emerson tried to hold on to my arm again, and I shook her off, hard enough that she landed on her butt. "Sorry. But you're not stopping me."

She didn't even try to get up. "Do you realize what you're doing?"

I didn't answer. I knew I was probably making a big mis-take. But I felt like I had no choice.

I scooped Laila up in my arms and turned around to face Dr. Emerson. She was standing now, and not making any move to stop me. The Prius keys were on the lamp table by the door, and I picked them up. "I'm borrowing your car." Not looking back, I walked out, taking the stairs down, managing to get into the Prius without meeting anyone.

Laila lay scrunched across the backseat. Every ounce of my reserve was needed to not just grab her, cradle her, and tell her to hang on until I could fix everything. I'd known her less than a day. What was I thinking?

I called Jack's cell. He didn't answer, so I texted. He replied immediately. He was on the way home from the hospital with a cast on his leg, his dislocated shoulder in an official sling. His mother had banned any phone calls. Luckily, Jack was a covert texter.

I texted him an update, ending with telling him I was heading to TroDyn with the girl.

His reply: Have 2 b the hero?

Yup

Gonna end badly

I hit the REPLY WITH COPY button: Yup

But u dont care

Nope

Hope shes worth it dude

My thumbs were poised over the keys. Then I typed: Me too

Be smart. Cant save everyone. Maybe u cant save her

I can try. Have to!!!!!

I snapped my phone shut and slipped it back into my pocket. Maybe she couldn't be saved by me. By anyone. But I had to try. I couldn't live with myself if I didn't at least try.

I started the car and backed out. Shifting into drive, I was just about to press the pedal when Dr. Emerson appeared in front of the car, blocking my way. When she saw I wasn't going to move, she walked around to the driver's side and opened the door. "I'll drive," she said.

She saw my hesitation, that I didn't trust her. She rested a hand on my shoulder. "I don't agree with this. But I don't want to see her die either."

I climbed in the back, my legs stretched out between the bucket seats, and put Laila's head in my lap as we headed toward Melby Falls.

I couldn't help but wonder about my mom, her connection to Laila. What was it? There was so much she had known all along and hadn't told me. She'd known about Laila and the others, what they were. Is that why she couldn't live with herself? Why she drank herself into a stupor whenever possible? Was she one of the scientists who worked on the project? Was she going to have me, and that's why she left? She didn't want me in the project?

My whole life I thought it was me. My scar. Her guilt over not being able to protect me from Packer that day.

Laila's eyes opened and she locked onto my gaze. "What's going on?"

I couldn't bring myself to tell her we were going to TroDyn, so I simply said, "We're getting you some help."

The corners of her mouth turned upward and she reached

a hand to my face. Her touch was warm, and goose bumps rose on my arms. Her voice was low. "Thank you." Then her eyes shut, but her hand stayed on my face for another moment before dropping back to her side.

There was no way out until I saw it through. Saw Laila through to whatever end there might be. And the end seemed to be pointing toward TroDyn. Laila rolled over, her arm reaching back, exposing the tattoo on her arm. I lifted it up. "What do you know about this tattoo?"

Dr. Emerson looked in the rearview mirror. "Just an identifier. The Karner Blue butterfly. Do you know about them?"

"Yeah, a little." I didn't mention I'd first heard of them only a couple of hours ago.

"You know they're completely dependent on one plant, the wild lupine?"

I nodded. "They're losing their habitat."

She said, "Yes. The tattoo of the Karner Blue is kind of a metaphor. For humans? We depend on food, that's it. This earth is our lupine. And we're killing it. One day soon, our habitat will disappear, and our food with it, just like the lupine is disappearing for the Karner Blue."

"So the tattoos are a reminder?"

She nodded. "That what we were working on, the auto-troph project, was in essence making sure we knew how to live without our lupine before it's all gone."

"You all have them?"

She shook her head. "No, just the . . . autotrophs them-selves."

Then why did my dad have a blue butterfly tattoo? Coincidence? A different species—not a Karner Blue? I thought about seeing Laila's tattoo the first time, right after I'd woken her at the Haven. "Hey."

Dr. Emerson raised her eyebrows. "Yes?"

"Well, when Laila first spoke to me, at the Haven of Peace, she was scared. She was convinced someone was going to find her."

A corner of her mouth raised. "She wasn't wrong."

"No, I mean a specific person. She said, 'The Gardener will find me.'"

The corner of Dr. Emerson's mouth flinched just a little at the name.

"What?" I demanded.

"The Gardener is head of the autotroph project."

So it hadn't just been from the book. The Gardener was real. I wanted to know something else. "She was so afraid when she said it. Should Laila be afraid of the Gardener?"

Dr. Emerson looked out the front window, her eyes distant. "We should all be afraid of the Gardener."

THIRTEEN

WE TRAVELED THE REST OF THE WAY IN SILENCE, AND I WON-
dered if the food situation was all that dire. There was so
much technology, so much we could create from nothing.
Could food really run out? I knew there was hunger, starvation even, in other parts of the world, but Melby Falls seemed
so far away from all that. I mean, wasn't there astronaut food
we could all eat or something? By the time food ran out,
wouldn't they have invented a pill to replace food?

When we neared Melby Falls, I sat up taller, feeling my
stomach clench. What was going to happen when we got
there? The entrance to TroDyn was a half-mile stretch of
blacktop lined with large pine trees the entire way. I felt like
I was driving up to a private school, or an insane asylum.
But just as we rounded the last corner and headed toward a
huge gate, a familiar vehicle pulled forward and blocked
our way.

Dr. Emerson slammed on the brakes and I held on to
Laila.

I leaned over to look out the window, just in time to see
my mother striding toward the Prius, arms swinging. Mom
grabbed the handle, but the door was locked. She pounded
on the window with a fist. "Open the door!"

Dr. Emerson hit the lock switch. I heard a click, and Mom wrenched the door open.

She looked at Laila and me, then her eyes flitted to Dr. Emerson, widening. "You!"

My mouth dropped open as Dr. Emerson stared at my mom. She covered her mouth with a hand and looked at me in the rearview mirror. "That's your mom?"

I nodded.

She started to get out, but before she could, my mom reached in and slapped her, hard. Then slapped her again before spitting out the words, "How dare you show your face around here?"

The words took a few seconds to form. "You know each other?"

Mom stepped back and motioned for me to get out, while Dr. Emerson seemed content to stay seated. My mom helped me pull Laila out, then I lifted her up and stood, cradling her in my arms. "Somebody want to tell me what's going on?"

Mom was still glaring at Dr. Emerson, but she said, "It's complicated."

"How do you know her?"

Mom's eyes narrowed. "We worked here, together."

The air was so tense, I wanted to say something but didn't know what.

Dr. Emerson looked at my mom. "You kept him in the dark all these years."

Mom shook her head as she looked at me. "He knows there are things I need to tell him."

Dr. Emerson stepped out of the car. "We have a bit of a problem, wouldn't you say?"

My heart pounded. "Mom? What's she talking about?"

"Don't." My mom's voice shook as she pointed at Dr. Emerson.

Dr. Emerson gestured at the gate. "We're here and he's determined to go in. Do you seriously think this is going to happen without his finding out?"

My arms began to tremble under Laila. "Finding out what?"

Just then, an alarm sounded and the gate opened slowly, both sides swinging outward.

Dr. Emerson set a hand on my arm. "You don't have to do this."

No matter what I was about to discover, there was no way I was just going to let Laila die. Maybe I would find out her life was worse than death, but I wanted to know for sure before I made a decision like that. And part of me hoped she would perk up, be able to decide for herself. Until then, I was going to do everything to keep her alive. Even if it included seeking help from TroDyn. So I shook my head at Dr. Emerson. "We're going in."

She backed toward the Prius as her eyes went toward the gate and the buildings beyond. "I won't go in there. I can't." Getting back in the vehicle, she said, "I'll wait, though. You won't like what you find."

Her words sounded way too certain for me.

Mom stood between me and the gate. "I can call someone to take her in."

My arms tightened, bringing Laila closer to me. If she were conscious, would she go along with this? Or would she feel I was betraying her by taking her to the one place she wanted to get away from? I asked, "Will they help her? Really?"

"If you're asking if they'll keep her from dying, yes." Mom's gaze hit the ground and stayed there.

I said, "There's a *but*, isn't there?"

"But it's not a great situation." Her eyes met mine. "Mason, if you go in there, you won't want her to stay. Even though she has to. Which is why you should just let me get someone to take her. And then we can go."

Maybe getting out of there was the best option. I could just leave. I already found out I couldn't help her. I did what I could, but someone else needed to save her. Or maybe there was more to it. Maybe the answers I was seeking lay beyond the gates.

Hitching up Laila in my arms, I headed toward the first building inside the gates. Mom ran up beside me, her hand on my wrist. "Mason, just give her to them. You can't do any more for her!"

"And why should I listen to you, after everything you've kept from me?"

She let go of me and stopped. "Maybe you shouldn't. But if you go in there, you'll find out. . . ." She sighed. "Believe me, your life will become much harder to live."

I stopped and turned around. "Is that a threat?"

"No." Her voice was soft and she looked small and sad. "It's a promise."

Dr. Emerson called out, "Your mother is right."

I ignored Dr. Emerson as I said, "Mom, I just need some answers." Walking backward, I watched her for a moment, before resuming my approach toward the entrance of TroDyn.

"Wait!" Mom ran up beside me. "I won't let you do this alone."

My head nodded back toward where Dr. Emerson waited. "She was afraid to come in. Why aren't you?"

Mom looked toward the entrance. "I haven't been here since . . . for a long time." She raised her chin. "But I hope I still have an ally or two."

The double doors opened, and two people in green hazmat suits stepped out, their faces obscured by hoods with dark glass masks.

Mom grabbed my arm.

I nodded at them. "Hey there."

They strode toward me, and as I tightened my grip on Laila, I stepped in front of Mom. "I just want to get help for her."

One of the people reached out for Laila, but I hesitated. What would happen if I handed her over? Would they let me go in, find the answers I was seeking? Or would they kick me out, leaving me even more in the dark than ever, unless my mom decided to tell me everything. But I still wouldn't know what happened to Laila. Plus, I had the feeling there was more going on than even Mom knew.

"No." I looked from one to the other. Neither came close to being my size, and despite their anonymous bravado, they seemed content not to confront me and test my physical strength. "I'm carrying her or she's not going in there."

They looked at each other for a moment, then turned back to me. One stepped aside and motioned that I should walk in front of them. That first step seemed to take about an hour, but then I found myself moving toward the door, escorted by one of the green people. And I heard my mom squawk.

Whipping around, I saw the other green person with a hand in her chest, shoving her back toward the gate.

"Let her go!"

Mom's arms windmilled as she fell backward on the ground with an "Oomph."

"I said let her go!" But with Laila in my arms, I couldn't help. My escort stood next to me. Could be that he, or she, was waiting for me to decide, maybe knowing I was torn between helping my mom or helping the girl in my arms, maybe thinking it was a way to get me to hand her over.

I swallowed as I watched my mom get up and try to fight her way back toward me, past the green person. My arms tightened around Laila as I wondered what would happen if I set her down. She might be snatched up, taken out of my sight as my mother and I were shoved out the gate.

"Mom!"

Her hair had fallen out of its ponytail and hung around her face as she stood with her hands on her knees, panting from the shoving match. She was overpowered, but as she looked at me, the message in her eyes was clear: She wouldn't give up.

Never before had I been forced to choose who to help. And now that the choice lay before me, I realized it was a type of triage I'd never planned for. My eyes rested on Laila's peaceful face, which seemed even paler than before. Her life was at stake.

Then I looked at my mom. How long since she'd put up such a fight? I'd never seen it before. For the first time in my life, I knew she had it within her to save herself.

"Mom, it's okay. I'll be okay."

Still breathing hard, she cried, "Please don't go in there. Please just hand her over out here and we can go home!"

"Mom . . ." I shut my eyes for a moment, giving myself the opportunity to change my mind. But when I opened them and took in the green suits, my mom looking fierce and disheveled, and lastly, the limp beautiful girl in my arms, my choice was solid.

Then suddenly, Mom ripped free of the green person's grip and ran toward me. "Just set her down! Let's go, she doesn't need you."

A flash of green beside me intercepted my mom and threw her to the ground.

"Stop! Leave her alone, I'll do what you want."

The green person released my mom and stepped back. Waiting for me?

I pleaded with my mom. "Please, I don't want them to hurt you. Just go. I need to do this."

Mom yelled, "Wait! I need to tell you something! Mason, please . . ."

And I stepped through the doors of TroDyn.

The person in green didn't say anything as the doors shut behind us, so I didn't even notice I was standing alone until I turned around. I was in a hallway with white walls, white tiled floors, and only one set of doors in front of me. As I started toward them, suddenly they were flung open and a woman stepped through, marching toward me. Wearing a pair of khaki pants and a white button-down blouse, she was fairly tall, sturdily built, and her blond hair came to her shoulders. She could have been anyone on the street, but for her face. She had this look. I mean, put a black-and-gray wig on her and she was a ringer for Cruella de Vil.

"Well." She halted a step away from me, shaking her head as she looked at Laila. "I didn't appreciate the last twenty four hours."

Did she want me to apologize? Because I wasn't about to. I opened my mouth to speak, but she held up her hand. "I wasn't talking to you."

Laila moved in my arms and I saw she was awake.

The woman said, "I was talking to my daughter."

My mouth dropped.

The woman raised one eyebrow.

Was *she* the Gardener? No wonder Laila had been so frightened. And then I saw a faint resemblance, same blond shade to the hair, the height, and the eyes.

Straightening up to make myself as tall and imposing as possible, I said, "She needs help."

"Oh, I know, I know." The woman patted me on the

shoulder. "How nice of you. It would have been nicer to just let your mother handle it at the Haven of Peace, but now you've brought her back, so all is fine."

"You know my mother?"

"Of course. And I know you. Too bad she chose to take you out of here when she did. You'd still have your face and who knows? Maybe you and Laila would have been coupled."

Trying to take in the implications of that piece of information, my eyes narrowed. "Laila needs *help*."

She shook her head slightly. "No, she doesn't. Not help. She needs to return to where she belongs, that's all. And she'll be fine."

I heard a click on the tile behind me, and I turned just in time to see a hand coming toward me, holding something silver. Stars burst in front of my face as I started to fall.

FOURTEEN

Although I didn't remember hitting the floor, the throbbing in my head certainly served as proof. I groaned as I cradled my temple, and my eyes fluttered, trying to focus. I'd watched reality cop shows a couple of times and was pretty sure I'd just encountered a Taser. A lump had definitely sprouted on the right side of my head, and I checked out the rest of me. I was still dressed, boots on my feet. As I sat up, I looked around at my surroundings. The small room was well lit, with wood-paneled walls. I was on a bed with a soft white down comforter, but there was also a desk and matching chair, and a blue recliner that faced a small television.

The lock in the door clicked, and I retreated to the edge of the bed.

Laila's mother walked in. She smiled. "You're awake."

"Where's Laila?"

"She's fine."

They got what they wanted, they had Laila back. "Why am I still here?"

"You wouldn't be, if it were up to me. I'd have put you outside with your mother and sent you on your merry way."

"Why didn't you?"

"Because the Gardener would like to see you."

My jaw dropped. "I thought *you* were the Gardener."

She tossed her head back and laughed. "Me? Oh no. I'm Eve." She held the door open and tilted her head. "Come on, Mason. Everything will be explained."

Eve waited for me to go through the door, then followed me into the hallway. "This way." She started to walk.

I followed. What else was I going to do?

The hallways were bright. The low ceilings were lined with fluorescent lights, the walls were white. Her heels clicked on the tile floor. We walked about a hundred yards before we came to a door. She held it open for me and I entered a room painted green, but this one had a couch and was covered with bookshelves, filled from end to end with books.

"You must be hungry."

Before I could stop myself, I said, "Starving."

"Well, some of us still eat around here. What can I have the cooks make you? A sandwich?"

"Yes, please."

"You can have anything. Tuna, bologna, chicken salad—"

"Yes, chicken salad."

"Wheat? White? Rye?"

Was this Denny's or what? "Wheat."

After she left, I tried the door. Locked.

I looked around and started reading spines. *The Jungle Book,* the Lord of the Rings trilogy, *Charlotte's Web*, *Oliver Twist*, every volume of the Oz books. Even the Five Little Peppers series, one of Mom's favorites. She'd read to me from her ancient copies when I was little. Then I stopped browsing and looked around, trying to figure out how many books the room housed. A lot.

"I have many books."

I spun around, expecting someone to be standing there. But I saw no one.

"Sorry to startle you."

The voice sounded canned, laced with an echo, almost disembodied, so that I couldn't tell it if was male or female. I followed the sound to a window near the side of the room. But when I got there, I saw it wasn't a window but more like a mirror on my side.

"I'm sure you have many questions. I'd like to answer them all."

My hands touched the glass. "Who are you?"

"Some call me the Gardener."

My breath caught in my throat as I struggled hard to not show my fear. I swallowed. "Why can't I see you?"

"You will. You will. I just . . . prefer this way for now. My assistant will return shortly."

"Eve?"

"Yes."

It occurred to me that it was probably Eve herself on the other side of the glass, screwing with me. So I screwed with her. "She's scary."

"Yes, she is." I heard a low chuckle. "But don't worry, she answers to me. She'll be coming to show you around, then she'll bring you to meet me. I'd rather you see everything first, then I can explain."

I wasn't sure any of this could be explained, by Eve or

whoever it was behind the glass. "Why? Why do you want me to know?"

"Will you ever stop wanting to know about the girl?"

That question was easy. "No."

"So I can only assume you won't stop seeking the truth. Seekers are dangerous. And now I must go."

"Hello? Are you there?" I banged my fist on the glass, but got no response. The door clicked open behind me and a guy in khaki pants and white shirt set a tray on the table, then left.

I pulled out a chair as I slid the tray over. A huge chicken salad sandwich sat on a white plate next to a large glass of milk. My stomach rumbled. I knew I should be cautious. They could have done something to the food. But why? They already knew a Taser knocked me on my ass. They had ample opportunity to get rid of me if that was their plan.

Reaching out with one hand, I hesitated, but only for a second, before grabbing the sandwich and taking a massive bite. Delicious. I devoured the sandwich and drained the milk, even licked the plate clean of wayward patches of chicken salad. There was room in my stomach for about three more of those sandwiches, but I shoved the tray away just as Eve returned and motioned for me to follow her.

"Nice timing." I was pretty sure she had been behind the glass, but I decided to play along.

As we walked down the hallway, I tried to orient myself, keeping track of lefts and rights. Not that it would do me a lot of good, other than getting me back to the green room with the books. I had no clue where to go from there.

Eve walked fast, but I had no trouble keeping up. A humming grew louder as we reached a pair of double doors so tall I would have had to jump to touch the top, and wide enough for a good-size car to drive through. She set both hands on the silver bar, like she was ready to push, but she paused. Turning just enough that her profile was visible to me, she asked, "Do you frighten easily?"

Now, there was a question I'd never been asked. "No," I replied, although I had to work hard to keep my voice steady.

"Excellent." She pushed the door open and stepped forward. "It would be best to stay very close to me."

As the door opened, the humming intensified into a buzz as a rush of warm, moist air hit me, along with a bright, blinding blast of light and the smell of flowers. Shielding my eyes with one arm, I stepped inside the room. The surface under my feet was cushioned, almost bouncy. Squinting up, I saw the ceiling was about twenty feet high, made of bubbled glass. And as my eyes adjusted, I saw the room was easily the size of a football field. But the sheer enormity of the room wasn't what stopped me in my tracks. The occupants of the room did.

I held my arm closer to my eyes as I blinked, trying to figure out if what I saw was real. Rows and rows upon more rows of kids—some looked my age, some younger—all sitting on the floor, their eyes closed and their necks bent back, faces turned upward toward the light. Small monitors sat in front of each one, a brilliant blue emanating from every blank screen. Each kid wore some sort of tight green bodysuit that covered almost all their skin. But the material was thin, so thin I could almost see through it, but not quite.

Were these people?

Eve stepped closer to the first row of them, beckoning me to follow. Peering at the kid nearest me, my eyes ran gradually from his face, pale in the sunlight, but luminous, almost sparkling. There was no expression, yet he seemed placid. I gazed at the other faces around him, all bearing the same expression, sort of a blank serenity, an outward satisfaction that didn't seem to go any deeper. My gaze left their faces and went back to the first kid, down to his chest and arms and crossed legs—

And then I saw it. Each kid was on a raised platform, about six inches off the floor, with a hole beneath. Snaking up from the hole were clear, shiny tubes that showed a green liquid inside. And the trail of the tubes ended inside the back of the kids' legs, into holes the same circumference as the awful scars on the back of Laila's legs.

I was in a garden. A garden of humans.

I must have gasped. Eve grabbed my arm and squeezed, shushing me, but I couldn't help it as the words fell out of my mouth in a near shriek. "What have you done?"

Slowly, as one, every kid in every row as far as I could see turned their heads toward me. Their eyes were so dark they seemed black, even in that bright light, and the buzz of the room became louder and louder, making me cover my ears as I started to back away. With an echoing click, the light went out. All those eyes, still focused on me, shone in the dark, their skin reflecting enough light to reveal movement as each kid, again in unison, reached out an arm toward me.

Something brushed my ankle and I screamed like a girl. The buzz filled my head.

Eve yanked on me, her nails digging into my arm as she pulled me toward the door. Her whisper was vicious. "Shut up, will you!"

And I managed to keep my mouth shut as she backed us through the doors and closed them, cutting off the buzz and turning it back into a mere hum.

She let out a deep breath before turning to me. "Did I not ask you to be quiet?"

"No, you didn't!" My hands were shaking and I leaned against the wall to keep from falling. "You asked if I frightened easily. You could have given me a few details before you showed me that—"

With one trembling finger, I pointed toward the door, half scared it would open up and those kids would start piling out, one after another, hands reaching out for me. "That place. Holy crap, what is that place?"

"The Greenhouse."

My hand flew over my mouth. The Greenhouse. Was that where Laila had been before Haven of Peace, the place she could remember only in snippets? My knees bent and I slid down the wall, slumping on the floor as I sank my head into my hands. I couldn't breathe, I couldn't think, as I imagined Laila in there among those kids. But I had to know. I had to know everything.

"What are those kids doing in there?"

Eve's hands fluttered a bit before she said, "Essentially, they are saving the human race. In fact, they are the future of the human race."

"How can you say that?" The picture of them all turning to me in unison, eyes dark, faces expressionless yet sinister at the same time . . . "They're not human." They couldn't be.

Eve tsked. "They are as human as we are. They simply have enhancements that we do not. Enhancements that will help them survive the disasters that are sure to leave you and me as dead as dust."

"But how could you do that to Laila?" My eyes narrowed. "Your own daughter. How could you?"

"How could I *what*? Do all I can to ensure that she survives what the entire current human race cannot?"

"No." I put a hand on either side of my head and squeezed my eyes shut, trying to get a grip. "No." Eve was insane.

Opening my eyes, I asked, "How could you put her through that, make her live like that?"

Eve shook her head. "You don't understand." She gestured at the closed door. "You see only the surface, the outside. Clearly, you have no idea what's going on underneath."

"Yeah, *clearly*." Getting my feet under me, I stood up. "I may have no idea what's going on underneath, but the outside looks pretty frickin' messed up. How many kids are in there?"

"These are all questions you should save for the Gardener."

"Bull! You're the Gardener! That's why Laila was so freaked out by *The Runaway Bunny*. Her own mother is the Gardener."

Eve rubbed her neck as she watched me, and her expression changed from defensive to something else. "I'm not the Gardener."

"Prove it."

"Fine." She turned and headed back the way we had come. When I didn't do anything, she stopped. Without looking back, she said, "You may want to follow me."

Glancing at the double door, I shuddered as I caught up to Eve and followed her down the hall. On the way back to the room with books, she took a left where we should have taken a right, and I lost my bearings. But there was nothing to do about that, so I quit trying to remember the lefts and rights. Which gave me a chance to ask questions about what I'd seen. "In the Greenhouse, what is that light?"

"Sunshine, perfectly replicated."

"Their faces looked like they sparkled."

She stopped before a door and turned to me. "Their clothing covers everything but their hands and faces, and for those we use a sunscreen, made of calcium carbonate crystals. Ultraviolet and infrared rays are deflected, but photosynthetic ones are not. A form of it is used in Australia for fruit crops that get damaged by the sun. Once testing is done in the U.S., it will be a big seller for TroDyn."

Nice, use humans as guinea pigs before fruit. "How handy for you."

Her hand rested on the silver knob. "Here we are. The Gardener is waiting for you."

Maybe my earlier gut reaction had been wrong about Eve. Maybe she was only what she said she was, the assistant. But I was sick of the runaround. I just wanted answers, no matter how horrendous they were. "Is it the person behind the mirror again?"

"No. You'll be meeting the Gardener, face-to-face." She tilted her head slightly. "Personally, I think you are nowhere near ready for this. But it's not up to me." And with a quick twist and push, she opened the door.

Even though my heart was pounding, I thrust my chin in the air and walked into the room. There was nothing extraordinary about it; it looked like a reception area. A red couch sat in front of one wall, while the other wall was one big mural. On the opposite side of the room was another door, and I wasn't sure whether I was supposed to walk through it or not.

Deciding to wait for further instruction, I paused to look at the mural.

The painting was of men on horseback. The first horse was white, its eyes and mane wild, and the man on his back wore a gold crown and held a drawn bow. Behind him was a red horse, again looking as untamed as the first, but its rider held a sword.

The third horse was black; its head was down, nostrils flared. The rider carried what looked like a pair of scales. And the last horse was a pale, greenish color, and seemed to be plodding as the others raged. Its rider was clothed in a white shroud and held a plain staff.

But that wasn't the part of the picture that disturbed me.

Underneath the four horses were scores of bodies, some of them still alive, reaching up, either to ward off the horses or plead for help. I couldn't tell which. And from the looks of those riders, if those people *were* pleading for help, they weren't getting any. Behind them all, the sun was an eerie red.

A buzzer sounded and I jumped.

The door opened slowly, mechanically. A hint for me to go through, I guessed. Taking a last glance at the mural, I walked to the door and held on to it for a moment. My hand shook and my heart beat faster.

As much as I wanted to find out the answers to all my questions, it took everything I had to take the first step through that door.

The first thing I saw was a platform, about two feet high, that went from one side of the room to the other. A massive desk sat on top, and behind the desk sat a man in a white button-down shirt. His skin was darker than mine, as was his hair, which was clipped very short, gray speckling the edges. He was handsome, with big striking eyes and delicate features.

A curtained window lay immediately behind him and, despite not really knowing my way around, I was fairly certain the green room with the books lay beyond the glass.

My gaze went back to the man behind the desk. He was

looking at me. No, not just looking. He was staring, studying, his eyes fixated so strongly that his forehead was wrinkled as he seemed to be trying to memorize me.

I could tell he was looking at my scar and, not really thinking, I reached up with a hand to cover it.

"Welcome. I'm Solomon."

Solomon. So unfamiliar.

"Your scar. Does it bother you?"

But that voice. So familiar.

"Not anymore. Not really." I swallowed. "I'm used to it."

"It's become a part of you."

"Yes." Where had I heard that voice before?

Then it came to me.

I staggered backward, grabbing for a chair.

I'd heard that voice for the first time when I was five, the voice I'd heard hundreds of times since then. Always reading *The Runaway Bunny*.

The man behind the desk, Solomon, was the man on the tape.

Solomon was my father.

And my father was the Gardener.

FIFTEEN

Words left me as I sank into a soft green chair at the base of the platform, looking up at the smiling man.

He said, "I'm glad to see you."

Nothing. Even if I could speak, what would I say?

"I realize this must be a bit of a surprise." He rubbed his chin, looking a little puzzled. Maybe he thought I'd gone mute or something.

I cleared my throat and sat up, trying to pull myself together. Although I wanted to, I couldn't come right out and ask—

"You're wondering if I'm really your father."

I nodded.

Solomon smiled. "Whether you want me to be or not, I am." He opened a drawer and pulled out a stack of pictures. He held one up. An eight-by-ten of me in sixth grade. He flashed a few others, all my school pictures. "Your mother sent them."

"But how . . ." I didn't even know what to ask.

"Your mother worked here, for me. And as sometimes happens when people work closely, they fall in love. Then she disappeared. Fortunately we were able to find her and bring her back."

I asked, "Why?"

"Why did she leave? She was going to have a baby, you, and didn't want anyone to know."

My voice came back. "Because she didn't want me to be part of the project."

He nodded. "She thought that I would force her to hand you over."

"Did you?"

His brow wrinkled. "Of course not. Do you think you'd be living as you are if I had?"

I shook my head.

"I loved your mother and respected her wishes. My only request was that she stay in Melby Falls."

Which made me wonder something. "Request? Or demand?"

"I'm no monster." Solomon drew in a deep breath and sighed. "I arranged for her job at Haven of Peace. I arranged for a monthly stipend."

The fund Mom kept talking about. She wasn't lying after all. "But you stopped paying that. I saw the notice."

He frowned, then jotted something on a piece of paper. "That's odd. I'll mention it to Eve and get it taken care of." He continued explaining about my mom. "She would still be part of the project, yet she'd have you to herself, to raise as she wished. Besides, I knew I couldn't be a proper father to you, eating breakfast, leaving for work, coming home to play catch in the backyard."

God, the times I'd wondered why I didn't have a dad to

do those very things. How many times had I asked my mom why I didn't have a dad like everyone else? I wanted to know. "Why? Why couldn't you?"

He held out one hand, palm up. "Because I was already committed here. My work was here."

"The autotrophs."

He nodded. "I couldn't let a family distract me from such crucial work. So the next best thing was to know you were close." He gestured to a shelf on the wall, filled with DVD cases. "Choose one." He pointed. "There's a computer over there."

Standing, I walked over to the shelves and ran my fingers along the unmarked cases and selected one. Popping it into the computer, I hit PLAY. Immediately, the sounds of cheering and screaming streamed out of the speaker as, filling the screen, was me, #45 in dark green, shoving #48 in black so the quarterback could slip through the hole to score the winning touchdown. Last year's league championship against Woodland.

"You watched my games?"

Solomon nodded. "Of course. Every one. You're very good."

On the monitor, the rest of the team left the sidelines and raced onto the field, surrounding me and the QB, all of us jumping and yelling at the victory. Before I could stop myself, I smiled. When the monitor went blank, I walked back over to the chair. "I have a tape of you, too." I wondered if he knew, if he remembered.

"I shouldn't have done that." His long fingers tapped the desk. "I suppose it was selfish of me, to want you to know who I was."

"But your face wasn't even on it."

"What do you mean?"

"The tape. It's just from your neck down."

"Well. I was never good at those things." He looked down at his hands. "I taped it myself, quickly, in a weak moment. I wasn't ever going to send it. . . . To be honest, I'm surprised your mother showed it to you."

She probably wouldn't ever have, if not for our neighbor's dog. I shook my head slowly, trying to focus. Such a simple answer to all my lifelong, complicated questions.

Mom, why don't I have a dad? Well, honey, he wanted you to be an experimental guinea pig and I didn't agree.

There it was, the absurd answer that explained my entire existence.

Holy crap.

With one hand I flipped through the stack of DVDs and read the labels. Every football game, every school program . . . So my entire life, my father had seen everything. He knew all about me.

I dropped my face into my hands as my shoulders slumped.

Worse, my mom *knew* that he knew me. How did you keep something like that from a kid? Especially when he's old enough to understand.

Maybe that was just it. Maybe the truth was worse.

No wonder she drank.

"I'm sorry, Mason."

"Don't!" I shouted into my hands, then looked up. Jabbing toward him with a finger, I said, "Don't talk to me like you know me. You don't know me any more than someone . . . someone who picked those tapes up off the street. Those tapes aren't me." I set a hand flat on my chest. "You don't know the first thing about who I really am."

His voice was softer. "I want to know."

I glared. "A little late, don't you think?" I turned around, not wanting to look at him. I was angry. Angry, still, with my mom for not telling me all this as soon as I got old enough to comprehend. Yet her hands *were* a little tied. Unlike my father, my mother did know me. And had she come out and told me my father was a mere two miles away, I wouldn't have just said, "Okay, cool. What's for lunch?" No. I wouldn't have let it drop. And the money. If I'd known about the money? I would have pushed to know everything, pushed to meet him, pushed to know him.

But what was his excuse? He'd given her no choice at all. Stay at TroDyn and they'd put me in the project, make me a human plant.

Wow, stellar option there.

Silently, I thanked my mom for getting the hell out, although it might take more time to get over all the secrets.

I whipped around. "Why couldn't you just have let her go? She could have gone anywhere and still made you tapes of me. Why did you make her stay in Melby Falls?"

He shrugged. "I hoped . . ."

"Hoped what? That she'd invite you down for Sunday dinner?"

"No." He shook his head. "I hoped for this. That, one day, you would come."

I flung my arms out to the side. "Well, here I am."

He started to speak, but I was done hashing it all. Nothing he said would get me to understand his view. And I had heard enough about myself.

"How did the tape of *The Runaway Bunny* wake Laila up?"

Solomon seemed taken aback at my question. Did he really think I'd be satisfied just learning about him and my mom? Learning about myself? I wasn't dumb.

"When her group was younger, we faced the same issues any parents face. One was getting them to go to sleep at night. They all needed to be on the same schedule in order for our control to be constant. So we hypnotically programmed them, with the books. One of the lines would put them to sleep. One would wake them up."

I thought of the others who were with Laila the first time I'd met her. "But why didn't the other kids wake up?"

"*The Runaway Bunny* was not their book." He must have noticed the confused look on my face, because he kept explaining. "The scientists who entered their children into the program needed to feel they were still individuals, despite being part of the larger group. So, when the children were little, their parents read the books to them before their naps and at bedtime. Each child had his or her own book that triggered them asleep or awake."

"And Laila's was *The Runaway Bunny*."

He nodded.

I wondered out loud. "So those books I saw in that room . . ."

"Each represents a child in the program."

"But there were so many."

Solomon shrugged slightly and started to rub his hands together.

There seemed to be so many more books in that room than there were children in the Greenhouse. "How many kids are in the Greenhouse?"

He met my glare. "Many. There are many."

"And they're all children of the scientists here?"

"Here, yes, and . . ."

"And what?"

He looked away. "Other places. Not everyone who is passionate about this issue is a scientist at TroDyn."

I still didn't understand. "How did you get all those people to just sacrifice their kids like that?"

His eyes widened a bit. "You're serious?"

I scratched my head. "Yeah. I don't get why they would do something like that."

Shaking his head slightly, he leaned forward, his chair creaking. "You're missing the big picture by seeing only the here and now. Have you heard of the Iroquois Confederacy?"

Other than knowing the Iroquois were Native American, I drew a blank, so I shook my head.

"They were a league of Native American nations, five at first, then six. It was the oldest democratic organization in the world. Some believe it was in place in the twelfth century, formed before Europeans even stepped foot on this continent."

I didn't get what, if anything, it had to do with TroDyn.

"The Iroquois Confederacy believed that any decision they made had to keep in mind how it would affect the seventh generation down the line."

Seven generations. I did the math. At that time, women probably gave birth younger, so perhaps around fourteen. "Even at only fourteen years to a generation, that would be about . . ."

"Ninety-eight years. They didn't make a decision without considering how it would affect people almost a hundred years later."

"But generations now are further apart than that. Some people aren't starting families until they're forty, so seven generations now would be closer to three hundred years."

"Exactly." He watched me. "Let me ask you this. How many generations ahead do you think our current government, all the world governments for that matter, are thinking when they make decisions?"

For a minute I thought about things that affected me, or would in the near future. The price of gas. That wasn't going down anytime soon. Global warming. That would only get worse. It seemed to me that governments weren't even thinking one generation ahead, let alone seven.

Solomon asked, "Do you ever wonder what kind of world will be left for you when you're, say, forty?"

Yeah, I did. I thought about that a lot. But I didn't tell him that; instead I said, "I don't get what this has to do with Laila. With the project."

He pointed behind me. "Do you see that?"

On the wall was a poster-size photo of a child. He was crying, tears glistening on his cheeks and running into his open mouth. Despite sticks for limbs, his belly was huge and he was in rags, any uncovered skin crawling with flies. I could almost hear the cry coming from his mouth, if he had strength enough to make any noise.

"That is part of your heritage, I'm afraid."

"What?"

Solomon cleared his throat and nodded at the picture. "That child is me."

SIXTEEN

"WHAT?" I GLANCED AT HIM, THEN BACK AT THE PHOTO. "Where?"

"The famine was in Wollo. My village in Ethiopia."

I didn't know what to say. First, I was stunned to find out that my ancestors, half of them anyway, came from Africa. I couldn't help glancing down at my arm and the color of my skin, a blend of his brown skin and my mother's paler hue. So much was explained in that brief moment.

He continued. "My family died. My mother, your grandmother, gave me any food she found, letting herself starve. Can you imagine what it was like, a child of five, watching your family perish, one after the other?"

My jaw fell. The child in the photo looked no older than two. I couldn't take my eyes off him. Nor could I wrap my mind around the idea that there was family in my past that I would never meet, that they were partly responsible for my existence, and I was never even on the planet at the same time they were. My eyes misted over.

Solomon said, "Of course, my life quickly improved. I was very lucky. That photo made the cover of nearly every newspaper in America, and offers of help poured in. An American doctor brought me and several others back to the

United States, and I never knew hunger again. Quite the opposite, in fact. I grew up in luxury." He paused. "But I never forgot."

His eyes glazed over for a bit, like he was somewhere else, seeing other things. Then he looked at me, focused once again. "Mason, have you heard of the Four Horsemen of the Apocalypse?"

I rubbed my eyes. "Sure, I mean, sort of." Then my head turned toward the other room, the first room. "The mural."

He nodded. "The four horsemen. Did you see the black horse? The rider with the scales?"

"Yes."

"Famine. The third Horseman of the Apocalypse is Famine. End-of-the-world kind of famine."

I asked, "You believe biblical prophecies? Aren't you a scientist?"

He raised his eyebrows. "I believe what I see. And I've seen famine, felt famine, like you could never imagine. You've seen it on television, probably, yes?"

I nodded.

"And wars?"

I nodded again.

"They just haven't been bad enough to end the world. But that day will come."

That seemed too doomsdayish to me. "But won't we have technology by then to combat famine? You know, like astronaut food, or we can go live on Mars or something?"

Solomon held his arms out to the sides. "Look around you. The polar ice caps are melting. As that happens, more and more carbon dioxide is released, speeding up global warming. How long do you think the world will hold out? Until we make a new Earth out of Mars?" He dropped his arms and shook his head. "We'll need an answer before then. Long before then, sad to say."

Despite holding an intense grudge against the man, I saw where he was coming from, his reasoning for wanting to create a human autotroph.

But I still thought it was crazy. "How will people, people living now, be able to get these abilities?"

"They won't."

"Then why do all this if you can't help anyone living now?"

He said, "That's exactly the selfish attitude most of the leaders of the world have. 'How will this affect us, what are we supposed to do?' et cetera, et cetera, et cetera. It's not about us here and now. It's about the future, and who will be here then. How they will take care of what we've left them." He shook his head. "And at this rate, we won't be leaving them . . . you and your generation . . . anything."

"So, what is your plan?" For me, it was always about one thing, the most important. "Who are you saving?"

"*Saving* is an interesting word. Are we saving anything? Maybe we're preserving life, ensuring that humans will be around after our current path would have seen us reach extinction."

That seemed like a strange way of looking at it. "But . . . isn't it a case of nature taking its course? I mean, if the planet is destined to be destroyed, shouldn't we just go along with it?"

He laughed. "That's so fatalistic. Why should we just give in to nature when we can do something to alter the path?" He tapped his fingers on the desk. "Mason, would you rather just be on the planet for a number of years, then once you're gone, it's as if you never existed? Or would you rather live forever?"

"That's impossible."

"Answer the question." He waited.

Thinking about it, I wasn't sure which way to go, what he wanted me to say. I mean, coming right down to it, wouldn't we all want to live forever? So although it was ridiculous, I said, "I guess forever?"

He smiled. "Exactly."

"But people can't live forever."

"No, they can't." He pointed to the DVD shelves again. "Bottom shelf, third DVD from the left. Put that in."

I half expected more football, but instead it was a savanna, and a male and female lion with cubs. As I watched, the male lion attacked one of the cubs, crushing its skull in his mouth. I watched with horrid fascination for a moment, then looked away and fumbled for the STOP button. "Why did he do that?"

"When a male lion takes over a pride, he kills the cubs of the previous leader, so the females will raise only his cubs. So only his genes will live on."

My eyes widened.

"No, no, no." He held up a hand and swished it in the air. "Don't worry, nothing like that is going on here. I'm trying to illustrate that it is within all of us to want to live on through our descendants."

"But that happens anyway."

He shook his head. "Not if famine and pestilence and war take over. We're all gone, and any possibility for descendants goes with us. Unless . . ." He paused.

Did he want me to figure it out? And then, in a flash, I did. I figured out the reason why those scientists would let their children be guinea pigs in an experiment to create a human autotroph. Because, if the world did indeed continue on its course, humans would be extinct. Unless there were humans who could survive famine. Humans who could survive to repopulate the world. Those humans, those genetically engineered descendants of the scientists, would live on. As would the gene pool of those scientists. That was what TroDyn, and the Gardener, my father, had offered them.

"They sacrificed their children for immortality."

He didn't answer right away. Then he said, "I don't like the word *sacrifice*. Their children are thriving and will be incredibly useful members of society, lead very productive lives here at TroDyn. Their lives will be instrumental to the future of the planet."

But what about Solomon? "You didn't feel the need to preserve your genes forever?" I asked.

Something flashed in his eyes that made me nervous. He said, "Had your mother approved, of course you would have been part of this. You would have had a hand in all of it."

Thanks, Mom.

I didn't say anything to that, had no idea what to say to that.

"You still could, you know. Be involved. I could send you to the best schools and you could come back here, help me run everything."

"My life would be set."

He nodded. "You'd worry for nothing."

For some reason, I didn't exactly feel the same joy Charlie Bucket felt when Willy Wonka offered him the chocolate factory. "What about Mom?"

He smiled. "I know she's been . . . troubled. You don't know her as I do—she's a brilliant mind and I'd be happy to have her back on the project. After all, she only left because of you."

The door behind me banged and I jumped.

Eve walked in, a glare on her face. "Getting caught up?"

Solomon snapped, "I asked you to leave us alone."

"And I did. For far too long, obviously." She gestured to me. "He may be your son, but you know next to nothing about him. *She* should never have been trusted with any of this. How can you just offer all of this, all of us, to him?"

How did she know? Then I looked at the curtained window behind the desk. She must have been sitting in the book room, listening to everything. And blaming my mother.

I stood up. "Listen, I want nothing to do with this place."

"You say that now." Eve turned to me, hands on her hips. "But wait. Wait until all the things he's been telling you start to happen. The wars, the pestilence, the famine. You'll be rattling the front gates to get in." She pointed up at the desk. "And he'll welcome you with open arms."

She dropped her hands and started to pace, talking to herself or to us, I wasn't sure. "I knew this was a possibility, always knew this was a possibility." She stopped to stare at him. "You haven't told him about Phase One, have you." It was a statement, not a question.

I asked, "What's Phase One?"

Eve crossed her arms and said to my father, "You tell him or I will."

Solomon looked furious. "What purpose could that serve at this point?"

Eve almost laughed. "You want to hand this over to him without telling him about Phase One?"

I repeated, "What's Phase One?"

Solomon leaned forward suddenly, like he was in pain.

Eve walked up to the desk. "Solomon? Feeling poorly?"

He nodded.

She reached for a small brown bottle and shook a few pills into her hand. "Here."

He waved her away.

"You must."

He sighed and took the pills, then continued. "Phase One relied upon the concept that we could turn a human into an autotroph, no genetics involved. You see, I did, at first, think we could give humans the ability to be autotrophic as things stand, using the resources available."

"Like how the nudibranchs became autotrophic."

He nodded, a flash of pride in his eyes. I almost felt pleased that I'd impressed him. He continued. "So for nearly a decade we tried medications and salves and anything we could think of to apply topically, thinking it was all based in the skin, the body's largest organ."

I said, "But it didn't work."

"No." He ran a hand over his eyes, rubbing hard for a few seconds. "We knew we had to go deeper, work with the bloodstream. Change the very components of life itself."

"This was before . . ." I had trouble saying it. "Before the Greenhouse?"

He nodded. "We had only ourselves as guinea pigs at that time. And I couldn't ask anyone else to do it, so . . ." His arms reached up in a stretch and his sleeve slipped, revealing the tattoo.

I stepped closer to the desk. "Is that a Karner Blue?"

He frowned and looked at his arm. "How did you know that?"

"But Dr. Emerson said only the autotrophs had that tattoo." My hands began to tremble as my heartbeat speeded up.

Solomon nodded.

"But if that's true . . ." I forced myself to walk around the side of the desk, where most of his body had been concealed.

Under the platform, there was a hole in the floor, where a

cluster of silver wires twisted up. Where his lower body should have been was only more of the same, a twisted mess of silver wires, along with hoses that had a green liquid flowing through, which began where the top half of his body ended.

I gasped and stumbled backward until I hit the wall, where I held out a hand, wanting something solid to grab on to.

"It's true, Mason." With a hand he pointed to himself. "You are looking at the world's first engineered human autotroph."

SEVENTEEN

Eve said, "You're wondering how it happened."

I could only manage a nod.

"We started substituting part of his blood with photosynthetic agents, all organic, derived from plants. As his body adjusted to a certain percentage, we increased it, until the photosynthetic agents outweighed the blood."

Solomon interrupted. "But we made mistakes. We didn't realize that organic materials would break down. While I was able to photosynthesize, it took all my energy. So we started on Phase Two, raising the children to live with less and less food, trying to see if we could succeed with that before giving them any of the organics."

I asked, "Did it work?"

He shook his head. "We just couldn't get the organics to stop breaking down, so we ended Phase One and tried to reverse it—to rid my body of the photosynthetic materials. My bloodstream could no longer function without the substances it had become dependent on and the circulation in my legs was compromised." Solomon's voice was flat, with no emotion. "They became gangrenous. So now I'm forever hooked up to a machine that provides me with fresh organic material to replace the old."

"And you take medicine?" I glanced at the bottle of pills, still in Eve's hand.

She saw me looking. "He's been feeling weak lately. These help." Her tone bordered on defensive.

Solomon didn't seem that bothered by what the experiment had done to him. He lost his legs. And his son. But then, whenever I spoke about my face, it was easier to keep the emotion out, easier to hold the feelings at a distance. "Was my mom here then?"

Eve made some kind of weird huff, but Solomon ignored her. "Yes, it was soon before you were born." He gestured at the tubes beneath him. "She's the one who worked on this solution. But seeing me like this was . . . too much. Especially with you coming." He gestured at his lower half. "I'm afraid this has made me a bit of a recluse. I haven't left TroDyn for nearly sixteen years."

I moved back to the other side of the desk so I wouldn't have to see that anymore. "And Phase Two?"

Eve jumped back in. "We were able to improve the organics, fix the flaws. We couldn't use the new ones on Solomon—his body rejected them. But the children were introduced to them very gradually and, most likely because of their young age, they didn't suffer the same problems as Solomon. However, as they reached adolescence, we realized there needed to be an element of technology; the organics alone would not continue to effect change at the cellular level. So far, Phase Two of the experiment is working." Eve paused, and then said proudly, "We have fully functioning autotrophs."

How could she be proud of it all? What they'd done to those kids? "What happened to Laila? Why was she sick?"

Eve shook her head. "She wasn't sick. We've been sending small groups to the Haven of Peace for a while now, to see how they function away from the perfectly controlled environment of the Greenhouse. Of course we put them in a semi-sleep mode to conserve their energy. And they do require at least one other autotroph to be nearby. They draw energy from each other. So when she was by herself—"

"She was never by herself," I interrupted. "She was with me."

Eve set a hand on her chest. "Pardon me." She rolled her eyes, which pissed me off. "When Laila was not with another autotroph, she began to weaken."

I thought what she didn't say: *Especially when she was running around Portland.*

Eve said, "That's an element we're working on."

I asked, "Where is she now?"

"She's perfectly fine. I've taken her off the away group for now, she'll just be staying here."

My chicken salad sandwich, which earlier had seemed to be fully digested, was threatening to reappear. "Where is she?"

Eve stared at me. "You didn't see her earlier? She's back where she belongs."

I slapped a hand over my mouth, trying to keep from throwing up. Laila was back in the Greenhouse, in that horror house of freaks. "Take me to her!"

"I'm not sure how that would—"

"Then I'll go myself." In three long steps, I was at the door and heading through. Heated words between Eve and Solomon started up behind me as I entered the hallway and tried to figure out which way to go. Choosing to go left, I hadn't taken two steps before an alarm sounded, white lights flashing in time with the constant blare. I started to run, trying doors along the way. One was unlocked and I opened it, knocking over a mop with a clank.

A janitor's closet. Probably the first place they'd look. So I ran to the next corridor, took a right, and then turned the next corner and flattened myself against the wall. In seconds, I heard running footsteps in the first hallway, along with a door opening and, a little while later, slamming. The janitor's closet, I assumed. The footsteps continued, but in the opposite direction. For all I knew, the building was set up to detect people in off-limits areas, so the more I stuck to the well-traveled areas, the less chance I had of sticking out like a sore thumb. I ran back to the janitor's closet and slipped inside. They wouldn't check it twice, I hoped.

There was a small window, so when I heard more footsteps, I hid until they went past, then watched where they went. Eve must have set off the alarm, telling everyone I was heading for the Greenhouse. And I would just have to follow my chasers there.

Two more pairs of footsteps went by, and I peeked out fast enough to see green jumpsuits, not the white shirt and khaki outfit. So the big guns had been called out for me. Or big Tasers, I could say.

But I wanted to be able to find my way back, at least this far, so I started digging around. I needed something I could see, but that no one else would notice. Or if they did notice, would think nothing of. There was a canister of that orange powder the school custodians sprinkled on puke. Although the smell and its associations made me want to hurl, I poured some in my hand.

Slipping back into the hallway, I followed the sound of the footsteps through the hallway. Before every turn, I trickled a little bit of powder on the floor. I wished I had worn tennis shoes; my boots weren't so great to run in, plus they were loud. I had to stop once in a while to catch the sound of the footsteps over my own, but I managed to keep up, just far back enough to hear their footsteps yet not be discovered. As I paused behind one corner, waiting for the footsteps to get farther ahead so I could turn right, I heard footsteps behind me. Without thinking, I ran across to the opposite hall, hoping whoever was behind me would go where the others had, walking right past without seeing me.

The footsteps, walking, not running, came closer and I crossed my fingers. Shirking back farther down the hallway, I could just see the person turn right, not even looking my way.

Eve. Her face was red and her short hair all messy.

I flattened myself against the wall. If she looked my way, she'd see me for sure.

I waited until she had turned out of sight, then I jogged after her, pausing at each corner to drop some powder and make sure she was ahead. And finally I had to slow to a walk. She was certainly in no hurry, which said to me she was confident the green suits had done their work and captured me.

Just as I was about to turn right again, I heard voices.

Sliding down the wall to the floor, I sat on my haunches and peered around the corner. Eve and three green suits had their backs to me as they stood in front of a double door. The Greenhouse. They'd led me right to it.

Wiping my hands clean of the rest of the powder, I pulled my head back and caught my breath, trying to hatch a plan. Though I was bigger than any of the green suits, probably stronger, the possibility of them each having a Taser was pretty high. My best chance was to surprise them, hopefully steal a Taser from one, and get inside the Greenhouse to find Laila.

Eve was the wild card. Something urged me not to underestimate her.

Taking a few moments to gather my wits, I leaned closer to see if I could catch a few words.

Eve said, ". . . talked about . . . timing . . . distraction."

One of the green suits, a man, spoke. ". . . not sure . . ."

Another green suit, also a man, sounded ornery, and it was easier to hear him. ". . . move on it . . ."

What were they talking about?

Eve spoke again. She was agitated, her voice was louder. "We are so close! Once the Gardener is gone, they'll have no choice but to side with us."

How could Solomon possibly go anywhere in his condition? I swallowed. Although I'd known her for only a little while, I got some serious evil vibes from her. Was she implying she was going to get rid of him?

I inched a bit closer, trying to stay out of sight, but I wanted to hear. Sounding impatient, Eve said, "I don't have time to wait around for that kid. He's going to screw up my plan. You two, split up, start looking other places. He didn't know his way around, he could be anywhere. You stay here. Taser him if he shows."

I listened to the footsteps recede before I looked around the corner. Down to one green suit, and his back was to me. Walking as softly as I could, I came up behind him. He heard me at the last second, but I threw an arm around his neck and grabbed his hand as he went for the Taser. He fought, kicking and trying to hit me with his other arm. He wasn't so tough once the Taser was out of play, and no match for me. Although I knew it was risky, I tightened my grip around his neck until he stopped fighting, and then I released him. He fell to the floor. With a trembling hand, I checked for a pulse, relieved to find he'd just blacked out and I hadn't really hurt him.

Looking each way, I reached out for the silver bar on the door and pushed. Like last time, the warm moist air hit me. Stepping inside the Greenhouse, I let the door shut. It felt as if I'd gone deaf, because immediately the alarm could no longer be heard. My heartbeat sped up and my breaths came faster.

The lights were out.

I forced myself to take a few steps and tried to focus. Although it wasn't pitch-black, it was hard to see. Soon my eyes adjusted and I started to see heads, rows and rows of them. I didn't want to get any closer to them than I had to, but I needed to see their faces.

Their eyes were shut.

I started to walk along the rows, looking for Laila. The effort was pointless. Their pale, glittering faces all looked the same. In the dark like that, I could have looked forever.

So I took a deep breath and called out in a loud whisper, "Laila?"

Nothing. None of them even moved.

Again, a loud whisper. "Laila?"

Nothing.

I said it slightly louder. "Laila?"

Then I said it in my normal volume. "Laila."

And I heard a faint reply. "Mason?"

I couldn't tell where it had come from, so I called out louder. "Laila?"

"Mason."

Definitely farther back in the room.

I took a step and nearly tripped. As I reached out to right myself, I brushed a clammy arm. "Ah!"

I jumped back.

Get ahold of yourself. Taking another step toward the back of the room, I called out, "Laila!"

I heard a quiet "Mason" from the back.

"Mason." Another to my left. I faced the sound.

"Mason." I whipped back around to the front where that came from.

What the hell . . .

Leaning down toward the closest row, I said, "Laila?"

Every eye in the row snapped open with a glow. At once, from everywhere, like they were footballs being tossed in the air one after another, came mutterings of my name.

A high voice in front of me. "Mason."

To my right, a low voice. "Mason."

Female to my left. "Mason."

Behind me, a male voice. "Mason."

From everywhere they came, high and low, male and female, until they all blended as one, chanting in unison, "Mason. Mason. Mason. Mason."

"Oh god, stop!" I covered my ears as I backed up to the front, as far away from those glowing eyes as I could get. "Shut up!"

They were speaking as one, thinking as one.

How would I ever find Laila if they knew everything she did? They were like one, like some freaked-up plant version of the Borg from *Star Trek*, nothing individual about them—

I froze, remembering what Solomon had told me.

There *was* one individual thing about each one of them. And I prayed Laila would remember what hers was.

EIGHTEEN

I CUPPED MY HANDS OVER MY MOUTH LIKE A MEGAPHONE and yelled, "Once there was a little bunny who wanted to run away!"

The chanting of my name stopped.

Silence.

Come on, Laila.

Again I yelled, "Once there was a little bunny who wanted to run away!"

Please. Please. Please.

I felt tears at the back of my eyes, and a pit in my stomach, and my voice cracked halfway through as I yelled, "Once there was a little bunny who wanted to run away!"

Please.

And I lost it.

Over and over I yelled, "Once there was a little bunny who wanted to run away!" until my voice was hoarse and tears ran freely down my face. "Why don't you remember?"

A buzzer rang for a few seconds, then a mist began to fall. I held my hands out in front of me, catching the handfuls of glittery water that slowly dripped off my palms and onto the floor.

Slumping my shoulders, I lifted my hands to my face,

where tears mingled with the glitter as I realized it was over.

Then, from farther back, there was a faint female voice. "So he said to his mother, 'I am running away.'"

I dropped my hands. "'If you run away,' said his mother, 'I will run after you.'"

Paralyzed with hope, I waited.

Then it came, from far back and to the left. "'For you are my little bunny.'"

I smiled, wiping away tears with one fist as I walked toward her voice.

There was a slight murmuring among the others, repeating some of the words Laila had said, but it wasn't loud enough to drown her out. I speeded up to a jog, slipping now and then on the slick floor as I headed toward where Laila had to be, calling out the lines, each of which she answered.

It was crucial I find her before the line that would put her to sleep. And if that happened, I would never find her.

Running toward the back of the room, to where I'd last heard her, I was down to the last line I could say. My last chance.

Her last chance.

Our last chance.

So I stopped, took a deep breath, and said the first half of the line. "'If you become a mountain climber,' said the little bunny . . ."

I held my breath.

From just off to my left came "'I will be a crocus in a hidden garden.'"

I turned toward the voice.

205

Laila.

There she was, her eyes glowing like the rest, face pale and sparkly, reaching out to me in the dark. I had never seen anything more eerie, or beautiful, in my life.

She was just a few yards away, but as I brushed past the others, they reached out, too, mimicking her, snagging my pants in their grips. Attempting to slap them away, I twisted and lost my footing. Then their hands were all over me, grabbing, as I crawled the last few feet. I reached out a hand toward Laila and she took it, not letting go until I was kneeling before her.

I held her face with both of my hands. "Are you okay?"

Tears slid down her cheeks, shining midst the sparkles. She nodded.

Putting our arms around each other, we embraced. I didn't want to ever let go, and from the strength of her hug—she was no longer weak—it seemed she felt the same.

A loud click sounded, echoing across the room, and a disquieting shudder ran through Laila's body. All around us, the others stirred as the mist of glitter stopped and the lights came on. I let Laila go and leaned back, shading my eyes with one hand. Only then could I see that Laila was seated on a platform, like the others.

As my gaze drifted down her body, the words bubbled up. "No, no, no. Oh no . . ."

Like all the others, she had the tubes with the green stuff going into her legs.

My father was the Gardener. He was responsible for this.

My hands went to the tubes, holding them. They were

warm. Repulsed, I wondered how to get them out of her.

She put a hand on mine, restraining me. "You can't. You can't take them out."

Around us, the voices started up. "You can't, you can't . . ."

"But I don't understand, how did they . . ."

"Don't." She shook her head as more tears spilled out. "It doesn't matter."

My words were babble. "But what do I do? I don't know what to do. I don't know how to help."

Laila touched my face. "There is nothing you can do."

I couldn't accept it, that the entire thing had been a waste. Jack getting hurt, my mom on the outside, possibly in danger, and Laila. Beautiful Laila.

There had to be something I could do.

The doors banged. In a flash, I pressed myself to the ground on my stomach, peering between a row of kids. Two green suits walked in, looking around. They reached the main aisle but didn't come any closer.

I wondered if they were as freaked out by the kids as I was. What if I hadn't seen Laila on the outside? If this had been where I first saw her, in a green bodysuit, glittering skin, hooked up to a machine like some alien, would I still have feelings for her?

Feelings.

I'd never had any feeling toward a girl other than a crush or confusion. Until Laila. I didn't know what it was. We'd been together only twenty-four hours, but when we were apart, I'd missed her so much it hurt. I didn't feel whole without her.

And lying there on my stomach, damp from the mist, wondering what would happen next, I felt more whole than ever. So I squeezed her hand. "Don't worry."

She squeezed back.

The green suits had a short conversation, then left the way they'd come.

I sat back up. There had to be something I could do for Laila. I said, "I'm going to get some help."

Laila frowned. "Help for what?"

I leaned forward and held her face in my hands. "For you."

Her eyes shut for a second, then opened back up. "I don't need help anymore. I'm strong now."

"But . . ." I looked around. "Look at where you are."

Her hands reached up to touch my face. "I'm where I belong."

"No." I shook my head. "I don't believe that. You don't belong here." My voice broke as I said, "You deserve a life. You belong with me. Don't you want that?"

"I shouldn't." Laila hesitated and her forehead wrinkled. "I should only want what I have here. That's what I'm supposed to want."

"But do you? Only want what you have here?"

Slowly, she shook her head as her hands pressed on either side of my face. "I want to be with you."

"Then I'm going to get some help."

She asked, "From who?"

"From someone I never thought I'd be asking . . ."

My father.

"I'll be back."

She smiled and placed her hands over mine. "Promise."

"Promise."

Although I didn't want to leave Laila, I knew she wasn't going anywhere. Or at least I figured she wasn't.

At the front of the room, I pushed the door open slightly and peeked out. The hall was empty, but the alarm still blared as the lights flashed. I hoped my little piles of orange powder were still there. I knew the first two turns without having to look, but then I had to stop. What had seemed like monstrous piles as I made them were actually tiny splotches of orange that required me to stop and look at every corner. I also had to listen for footsteps, not easy with the alarm going. Eventually, I saw the janitor's closet and went running into Solomon's quarters from there.

"Solomon!" There was no response. As I entered the room with his desk, he was visible, lying on the floor amid a growing pool of a green, viscous substance.

The organics were slowly draining out of him.

I skidded to a stop right before him, and fell to my knees. "Solomon?"

His eyes opened immediately and he reached out a hand. "I'm glad to see you."

"How did this happen?" But I knew, even as I asked.

"Eve." He clutched a small bottle of pills. "She's been poisoning me and I didn't even know. But now, with you here, she just couldn't wait for me to die. So she . . ."

I put my hand on his forehead, such a useless gesture. "What can I do? How can I help?"

He shook his head. "She's got some of them on her side.

I should have seen this coming. She stopped the payments to your mother. She's behind . . ."

His eyes closed as his head sagged to one side.

"I'll get someone to help!"

He swallowed before speaking again, his voice breathless and weak, so that some of the words dropped away. ". . . alarm . . . a lockdown. Everyone . . . in their quarters. Won't come out . . . until . . . all clear."

That explained the empty hallways. "I'll bang on doors, find someone."

He reached out for my hand and gripped it. "I need to tell you some things, things I never got to say."

"No!" I dropped his hand. "I'm going to find help!"

"There's no one to help. . . ."

But I knew someone who might. "Tell me how to get out to the gate where I came in."

He must have seen something in my eyes, because he didn't argue, just told me the way. With a shaky hand, he pointed to his shirt pocket. I reached in and extracted a plastic card.

". . . open the gate . . . locked doors." And those were the last words he said before he passed out.

I stood, looking around for something. I wished I had taken that green suit's Taser when I had the chance. Then I noticed the fire extinguisher, and the fire axe below it. Ripping the axe off its holder, I repeated Solomon's directions as I ran, hoping I didn't encounter anyone, because, at that point, I would use the weapon in my hands. In less than five minutes, I'd reached the front. I shoved the doors open and ran to the gate. *Please be there.*

NINETEEN

I yelled her name. *"Mom!"*

"Mason?" She stepped out of Dr. Emerson's Prius and ran over to me.

"Mom!" I found the lockbox for the gate and slipped the card inside. Three green lights lit up in succession and the gates slowly swung open. Mom slipped past them, and I held the axe out to the side with one arm as she hugged me. "Thank God. It's been hours. I was so worried."

"He needs your help. Solomon needs your help." I stepped back. "We have to go."

Mom paused. "He's your father."

"I know."

She didn't move.

"What?"

Then she pointed. "She can help, too."

Dr. Emerson stood by her Prius.

Not wanting to waste time arguing, or ask when they'd made up, I shouted for her.

As she jogged to the gate, she called out, "Is it Laila? What's happening?"

"I don't have time to explain. Please—we need your help."

She took a step back, hesitating. She shook her head. "I can't. I can't go in there."

My knuckles grew white from gripping the axe. "Not even for Laila?"

She shook her head and stepped back.

After everything? Everything with Laila, the rush to get to TroDyn? The words came out before I could stop them. "You suck!"

I didn't take time to see her reaction. Instead, I turned to Mom. "We have to hurry." And we ran for the front door.

Just inside, I pointed. "This way."

Mom said, "I know the way."

So I brought up the rear as we ran to Solomon.

Although he was obviously in bad shape, his eyes opened and his face lit up when he saw her. Mom knelt beside him and put a hand on his face, whispering his name over and over. As he came to, she started rearranging the silver tubes. "Who did this?"

Solomon swallowed. "Eve. Eve did."

Mom froze at the name. "Why in the world . . ."

I blurted, "She wants to take over. I heard in the hallway. And she's been poisoning him."

Mom shook her head. "I never trusted that woman." She continued to sort through the tubes.

It was a little weird, to see the mother who always seemed on the edge of losing it be so competent, like it was second nature to her. "Here. This needs to be connected now. I don't know if we made it in time." She looked at me. "Can you lift him back in his chair?"

With Mom on one side, we got Solomon back in his chair, and she started hooking him back up to all the silver tubes.

I asked, "What do we do now?"

Mom asked, "About what?"

I said, "Everything! The kids in the Greenhouse. Eve taking over." And, of course, the one thing I cared about the most. "Laila."

Mom shook her head. "Eve is crazy. And whoever she has on her side is crazy, too."

"But how do we stop her?"

Solomon seemed to be getting some strength back. His voice grew steadier as he spoke. "Eve has been lobbying for a long while now. She wants to make a deal with the military."

Mom bit her lip. "I can't believe they would go for that."

Solomon said, "Eve lied about it. The families think it's simply advancement in the project, a military intervention with a lot of funds that will speed our work along."

I recalled my conversation with Dr. Emerson, her worries about the project turning toward the military. Had she been talking about Eve? "So most of them have no idea their kids would become soldiers?"

Solomon shook his head. "Except for a few who share Eve's thinking, I doubt any of the others truly understand the implications."

"It's always been that way," Mom said. "The parents are blind, blind to everything but their cause. All Eve did was put it in a bigger, prettier wrapper, and they all went along with it." She patted Solomon's arm. "Behind your back."

"Oh my god," Solomon moaned. I was starting to see him in a different light. He honestly did want to save the human race. Was it possible, despite everything I'd seen in the Greenhouse, that he was the good guy in all this? And Eve the bad one, the one to blame?

I asked, "So? What do we do about Eve?"

Solomon grabbed my mom's arm. "You can't let her do this—"

"But she doesn't know you're alive, right?" I interrupted. "I mean, she meant to leave you for dead."

He nodded. "And it almost worked." He looked at Mom. "There are only a handful of people here who could have fixed the damage to me."

Solomon coughed. My mom found a towel and held it to his mouth.

I asked, "Can we shut this all down? End it now, forever?"

Solomon had stopped coughing and held the towel over his mouth. He and Mom exchanged glances.

"What?"

Mom held my arm. "Mason. You can't just shut this project down."

"Why not?"

She said, "You saw what happened to Laila when she was away from the others for just a day."

"Yeah. But you can't just keep them here. People know the truth. I know the truth. Jack knows the truth. We can tell everyone, get this place shut down."

Mom looked over at Solomon.

"What?" I nearly screamed. "What aren't you telling me?"

Mom cleared her throat. "Mason, I know you care about Laila, so think about this. If you were to call someone, the FBI, even Health and Human Services, what would they do?"

"What do you mean?"

Mom gestured toward the door. "The kids. What would they do with the kids? Think about it."

There had been stories on the news before, compounds full of religious freaks who married off young girls to grown men. Law enforcement had gone in and taken care of it. "They'd make sure they were okay, wouldn't they? Find them foster homes or something?"

Solomon's voice was ragged when he said, "These children cannot just be sent to foster homes. Law enforcement would not understand. They'd rip the children out of here with no clue how to care for them. They'd separate them all, try to force-feed them when they refuse to eat or drink. In effect, Mason? They'd all be dead before anyone figured out what was wrong with them."

No, it wouldn't go down that way. "The TroDyn scientists would tell them what to do!"

Mom said, "From jail? Sweetie, they'd throw everyone, including me, in the slammer and throw away the key."

My eyes widened. "Why you?"

"Come on." She tilted her head and laughed a little. "I knew about this and took care of those kids in the Haven of Peace for years. TroDyn has been making automatic deposits into an account in my name for fifteen years. If nothing else, I'm an accessory. And with me in jail, even if it's only for a little while, you'd be in the foster care system so fast your head would spin."

The thought of losing my mom, my home, maybe my entire way of life, made me ill. I dropped onto a chair. "So what do we do?"

Solomon spoke up. "First we need to quash whatever plans Eve has. We need to let the other scientists, the other parents, know what her plans are for their children. Let them understand that the project here is in danger if she takes over."

The alarm suddenly stopped.

I stood up.

Mom asked, "Where are you going?"

"To the Greenhouse. I've got to protect Laila."

Solomon shook his head. "You can't go there right now. We need to plan this out. I must deal with Eve myself."

I grabbed the fire axe and bolted from the room as Mom yelled for me to come back. I couldn't stay there, knowing something might be happening to Laila. Fortunately the orange powder was still in the corners, plus the route seemed more familiar than the last time. Three quick blasts of the alarm sounded as I neared the Greenhouse. I slowed to a jog, stopping at the last corner, before shoving open the door and stepping inside.

Eve stood near Laila with a couple of green suits. She turned to me. "You finally found it."

She thought I'd been running around all that time, looking for the Greenhouse. I nodded as I walked to them, keeping an eye on them as I tightened my grip on the axe.

Both green suits eyed the axe and brandished their Tasers.

"Can we dispense with the showing of weapons, please?" Eve pointed at Laila. "Say your good-byes, then you can be off."

What good-byes? I had no intention of leaving Laila. But Eve's tone was more ominous than the situation, no matter how unknown it was, called for. "What are you talking about?"

Eve said, "You had your chance." She turned to Laila. " 'If you become a crocus in a hidden garden,' said his mother, 'I will become a gardener and I will find you.' "

Laila's eyes dulled and her chin dipped down onto her chest.

I glared at Eve. Did she think I was an idiot? I quickly said, " 'If you become a mountain climber,' said the little bunny, 'I will be a crocus in a hidden garden.' "

Laila's head raised and she looked around.

Eve rolled her eyes. "Fine." She said something in a language that sounded like French, and Laila's eyes dulled once more, and her head tipped forward. Eve said, "She knows it in seven languages. Do you?"

God, I *was* an idiot. Holding out the axe, I crossed in front of them to sit beside Laila. I set down the axe and reached out a hand to hold Laila's head up.

"Just leave her. She's better off here now anyway." Eve straightened up, a faint smile on her face. "This project is about to come under new leadership."

My eyes narrowed. "Solomon won't let you."

Her eyes flashed. "Solomon has been holding us back."

She had no idea Solomon was still alive. And the longer she was in the dark about that, the better chance we had of stopping her. "Holding you back from what?"

Eve started to pace a little in the aisle. "TroDyn has power and money, yes. But who has more of each?"

I shrugged as I moved closer to Laila and let her head rest on my chest. At that point, I didn't care about whatever Eve had to say.

Eve stopped moving. "The military. With their power and financial backing, this project could go leaps and bounds beyond what Solomon, what any of us, ever dreamed."

To me, military involvement equaled point of no return, and I found myself caring again, fairly quickly. "But why would the military want to spend money to end starvation?"

Eve laughed so hard that a few tears came down her face. "That is priceless." She held her stomach, trying to stop laughing. "Oh my god, they couldn't care less about ending starvation." She pointed at me. "Don't you see the practical implications of this project? What military on Earth wouldn't give anything to have soldiers that require no food or water?"

It was one thing to hear Solomon talking about the possibility of what would happen if the military became involved. But Eve's reasoning made it sound like she had already cut a deal with them. "But what about Solomon? What he said about famine. Even the military will have to deal with famine."

Still smiling, Eve said, "Solomon was worried about the

wrong horseman. We need to worry about the one with the sword. War is going to end this planet long before famine does. I plan to be on the winning side." She nodded at Laila. "And I plan for my daughter to be on the winning side."

Although I'd known him for less than an hour, I was pretty certain of one thing. "Solomon will never allow it."

"Solomon, Solomon, Solomon." Eve crossed her arms. "Do you know how tired I am of hearing about Solomon? How innovative he is? How smart he is? Well, I'm done with that." She looked at the two green suits, then glared at me. "Plenty of us are done with that."

The double doors slammed open. Several people in white shirts and khaki pants walked in.

Eve waved a hand at them. "Didn't you hear the lockdown? You should all be in your quarters." She looked a little unnerved. Was it because she thought they might find Solomon? Find him and save him, like I hoped I had done?

A tall red-haired man stepped forward. He said, "The all-clear sounded a few minutes ago."

That must have been the three blasts of the alarm I'd heard.

Eve said, "Why are you all here?"

The red-haired man looked at the woman next to him, then turned back to Eve with a frown. "This is the first place we come after the lockdown drill." He held a hand out to his side. "To see how they are."

Eve shook her head slightly. "I knew that."

A man with a gray beard asked, "It was a drill, wasn't it?"

"Of course it was a drill." Eve stood up straighter. "And

I'd hoped you would all come here, actually. Please, gather round. I have an announcement."

Eve stepped forward, away from the row where we sat, and the green suits angled themselves in the aisle so they hid Laila's row, and me, from view. I had no desire to reveal myself at that point, because I had no idea what any of those people would do if they saw me. And I had no plan, either for waking Laila up or getting her out of there, or even getting myself out. So it was better to just lay low as long as possible.

Eve's voice was filled with emotion as she said, "Solomon is dead."

Several people gasped, and one of the women burst into tears. Murmurs of "How? When? What happens now?" grew louder.

I wasn't sure what would happen next, but I knew that those people thinking Solomon was dead would be dangerous to everyone.

So, taking a deep breath, I stood up, revealing myself to the group.

TWENTY

As their murmurs died down, I walked to the aisle, brandishing the axe at the green suits when they turned my way.

I cleared my throat. "She's lying."

Eve whipped around. "Don't listen to him."

"No!" I yelled. "Don't listen to *her*! She's been poisoning Solomon for months! She ripped out his tubes and left him for dead! I saw him!"

There were more gasps and murmurs from the crowd. Maybe they were trying to figure out who they should believe. Or maybe just which one of us was less crazy. And I kind of figured my yelling and waving the axe around tipped the scale toward me being the loonier one. My bad.

The man with the gray beard spoke as he pointed at me. "Who is that?"

A few people shook their heads, as did Eve, who said, "He kidnapped Laila from the Haven of Peace, and nearly killed her before he brought her back."

"That's not true!" As I found myself shaking the axe once again, I realized I had a much stronger weapon at my disposal. "I'm Solomon's son."

The murmurs grew to outright exclamations as most of

them stared at me, trying to figure out if I was telling the truth.

Eve said, "He has no proof."

Someone called out, "He doesn't need any proof."

The crowd parted and I heard a squeak as my mom stepped through, pushing Solomon in his wheelchair until they stood before Eve. There were relieved exclamations. While Mom looked directly at Eve, she spoke to the crowd. "He's my son with Solomon."

Then the gray-haired man spoke. "Is it true about Eve?"

My mom said, "It's true. Eve attacked him and left him for dead."

Eve took a step back. The green suits looked at each other, seemed to evaluate whose side they should be on, and moved away from Eve.

My mom continued, "But Mason . . . our son"—she pointed at me—"found him before it was too late. And then he got me."

Solomon said, "I'm already feeling stronger."

There were a few relieved exclamations, until the gray-haired man turned to Eve. "Why?"

Eve smiled. "You people have no idea. No idea how important this project is."

Mom frowned. "I'm quite certain they do."

Eve laughed as she reached down and pulled a knife out of her boot. Green sparkled on the blade. "The deal is done. Once I took care of Solomon . . ." She glared. "Let me rephrase. Once I thought I took care of Solomon, I called my contact with the military. They'll be here in twenty-four hours."

Gasps turned into shouts.

Eve knelt down to the closest child and sliced through one of his silver hoses. A green, viscous liquid spurted into the air as the child moaned. The others around him joined in, launching what sounded like a mourning medieval chorus.

Someone screamed. "I need you all back there," Eve said. With her head, she nodded toward the far back corner. "All of you, back there."

Slowly, we all moved to the back as Eve continued to hold the knife, standing slowly. "Make a move, and someone will die."

As Eve headed to the front, Solomon called out, "Eve!"

She turned as she backed toward the double door. "I'll lock you all in here until tomorrow."

The red-haired man yelled, "There are more of us out there!"

Eve smiled. "I'll simply tell them Solomon is dead. Or I'll tell them whatever I need to in order to stall them until tomorrow. When the military arrives, they'll be welcomed with open arms."

She pushed on the double door, still facing us as she paused once more. She started to say something, but just as her mouth opened, I saw a flash of red as a fire extinguisher hit her in the back, knocking her down. I ran with a couple of the men to the front. They restrained Eve as I looked to see who had delivered the blow.

Dr. Emerson held the fire extinguisher and shrugged when I raised my eyebrows. I said, "I'm sorry I said you suck."

With a clank, the extinguisher slipped out of her hand. She said, "You were right."

"Not anymore."

She smiled.

As people noticed her, they approached and greeted her. There must not have been any hard feelings about her leaving, because they all seemed pretty happy to see her. Even Solomon reached out to hug her.

A few people rushed to the side of the moaning child, as everyone gathered around, the gray-haired man clapping for our silence. "Solomon wants to speak."

Everyone went silent. Solomon said, "This isn't over."

I looked at Eve on the floor, surrounded by two green suits and three men in white and khaki. It seemed over to me.

Solomon continued. "I have no idea who Eve contacted, no idea how to stop the military from coming here. There's only one thing we can do."

People started to whisper.

The gray-haired man called out, "Project X?"

Solomon nodded.

A few people groaned; one of the women started to cry.

I asked Dr. Emerson, "What does that mean?"

She said, "I think it means they're moving."

"Moving what?"

She said, "You mean moving who. . . ." She waved a hand out at the kids. "Project X stands for Project Exodus. They're moving the Greenhouse."

"They can't!"

My mom came over to me. "Mason, they have to. Solomon cannot risk the children."

"But where? Where will they take them? How can they make another Greenhouse so fast?"

Dr. Emerson and my mom looked at each other. Dr. Emerson said, "Mason, this isn't the only Greenhouse."

"What?" And then I thought about it. The books in the green room, the books that each represented one child. There were thousands of books in that room. "How many Greenhouses are there?"

Solomon spoke up. "We have ten in the United States."

I stumbled. "You have some in other countries?"

Solomon nodded. "All seven continents."

Seven? How? My mind reeled. And then I remembered Laila. "Oh my god." As I ran to her, I called out, "I need somebody who speaks French!"

A kind woman with wire-rim glasses and blond hair spoke the French words as I told them to her in English. Laila blinked her eyes and looked up at me. "Mason?"

Holding her face in my hands, I planted my lips on her forehead, then held her, not ever wanting to let go.

Mom knelt beside me. "Mason, they have work to do. We have to go."

I shook my head. "I'm not leaving her."

Mom scratched her head. "You have to."

"I'll take her with me."

"You already know what that would do to her." Mom set a hand on my shoulder.

I leaned back, looking at Laila. Then I thought of something. "What will happen to Eve?"

Mom said, "She'll go with the others. They'll keep an eye on her, but I'm sure she'll keep doing her work. You know the saying, keep your friends close . . ."

"And your enemies closer."

"Exactly." She shrugged. "There is no other recourse. They can't just call the police and turn her in."

Laila said, "Where are they taking us?"

Mom shook her head. "That, I don't know. But you'll be safe."

Laila looked at me. "I want to stay with you."

I smiled. "I'd like that."

She put her arms around my neck and pulled me so close I felt her breath on my face. "Then let's do it. I don't care if I only live a little while. I want to spend my time with you."

I pressed my forehead against hers. I wanted so badly to say yes, to rip out her tubes and carry her out of there. Live all we could for as long as we could. For as long as she could.

Instead, as I felt my eyes tear up, I whispered, "Maybe they'll figure out a way for you to survive off the machine, by yourself."

Her arms tightened around my neck. "No. They won't. Take me with you."

My hands went up to her face and I leaned back. Tears started to spill out of her eyes as I felt my own start to slide down my cheeks. "I can't. I want to. But I can't."

"No." Her face crumpled as her eyes squeezed shut, and her head went from side to side in my hands. "No." She held me tighter. "Please. Mason, *please*."

"Listen, listen." Sobs reached my throat and I struggled to gulp them back down. "It will happen. They'll figure it out. And you can come to me."

Her brown eyes were filled with tears. "Where?"

Where would I be? Dr. Emerson said there was a chance of stabilizing the organics once the kids stopped growing. So maybe when Laila was eighteen? Nineteen? I would be out of high school. But where? "Stanford. I'll be at Stanford. You'll find me there." Oh, how stupid. She had no idea about Stanford. I reached into my pocket and thrust my phone into her hand. "I'll find you," I said. "I'll find you."

Before she could say anything, or before I could start bawling like a two-year-old, I tightened my grip on her face and leaned forward, touching my lips briefly to hers. When I drew back, her eyes were shut, her sparkly cheeks wet from tears. She opened her eyes and set both her hands on mine. Then she leaned forward and put her lips on my cheek, the one with the scar. She stayed there until I knew I had to move or I never would.

I whispered, "See you." Her hands clung to mine a few more seconds, then she let go, watching me. I stepped away and didn't look back. I couldn't. If I had, I never could have left without her.

As I walked toward the double doors, the entire place was in chaos. Many more people had come in, and no one even glanced my way.

My mom was with Solomon, who held out a hand to me. I took it. His skin was warm. "Mason," he said, "I'm glad I finally met you."

I nodded.

He said, "I have to leave. But I have an offer you should consider. I want to help with your future. Perhaps even be a part of it. In some way."

"I'll consider it."

I left my Mom alone to finish their good-byes.

I found my way outside to where the Jeep was parked, and leaned against the driver's-side door, wiping my nose with my sleeve. When my mom came out about ten minutes later, her eyes were red.

"You still love him," I said.

She nodded. "I always have."

"Then why did you leave him, leave here?"

One of her hands reached up to pat my face. "You have to ask?"

No, I didn't. Everything she'd done was for me. That was pretty clear. I started to open the car door and she shoved me a bit. "You're too young to drive."

I was still wiping away tears. "Since when?"

"Since now." Mom smiled. "Things are going to change."

We got in and headed for home. I asked, "Are you out of a job?"

She nodded. "Pretty much. But I'd been thinking about a career change anyway. I can teach at a college in Portland."

"Really?"

She nodded. "Free tuition for you."

As I looked out into the side-view mirror and watched TroDyn recede and disappear, I said, "No way. I'm going to Stanford."

EPILOGUE

"This is the end of the tour, you two." The pert and pretty brunette Stanford tour guide holds up a hand to stop us, and Jack is so busy watching everything but her hand, he walks right into me.

"Watch it," I whisper.

"Sorry." He shrugs.

The tour guide points out the commons. "Feel free to hang out here as long as you'd like; they have great iced coffee." She hands me a voucher. "Enjoy yourself, on us."

Jack continues to stare as the tour guide waves and walks away, so I grab his T-shirt sleeve and pull him toward a table.

He laughs and grabs the voucher out of my hand. "I'll go get us some snacks."

I sit down at the table and put my face up toward the warm sun. Our spring break road trip to Palo Alto is a welcome reprieve from the dreary Pacific Northwest winter. And a nice way to gear up for the end of our junior year. I glance at my watch. We have a half hour before I meet with the football coach. Since sophomore year, I added another twenty pounds of girth and two inches of height, so my football possibilities at Stanford are greatly improved.

Students are walking to and from classes as I wait for Jack, and I enjoy watching them. After a few minutes, I notice a girl with short platinum hair almost to her shoulders, standing with her back to me. Dressed in faded Levi's and a white tank top, she is reading the bulletin board on a kiosk in the center of the courtyard, about fifteen yards from where I sit.

The girl is tall, with an athletic build.

She seems so familiar, and I study her, every aspect of her.

The girl is tall. Tall enough?

I shake my head, trying to get a grip. It had been over a year since that day at TroDyn. I hadn't heard anything. From Laila. Or from my father. Although Mom finally revealed the details of my college fund. By scrimping, and not touching it all these years, she'd saved enough to pay for whatever college I chose to attend. Hence the big open arms for me and Jack on our campus visit.

Mom reassures me all the time that no news is good news. I assume bad news would make CNN.

Every day, I call my old cell phone with my new one. It always goes immediately to voice mail.

Still, I find myself drawn to the girl at the kiosk.

And then I am standing, taking a step toward her.

Her hair. Too short? Wouldn't it be longer?

I am only a few steps away, and I reach out for her. . . .

Jack clamps his hand on my shoulder, startling me. He says, "Dude."

Just then, a guy pops around the kiosk, gives me and Jack a funny look, then embraces the girl, saying, "Hey, Jen."

I clear my throat and look at Jack. "Yeah?"

Jack says, quietly, "It's not her. Not yet."

I nod. "I know that."

"Do you?"

My eyes widen in a mock glare. "Yes, I do." Then a corner of my mouth turns up. "Sue me. I can't help it."

We go back to the table.

Jack slides an orange tray over to me. I pick up a peanut butter cookie and take a bite.

Jack holds up a Yoo-hoo. "A toast?"

I grin and pick up the iced coffee from the tray, holding it to his bottle of chocolate milk.

Jack says, "To the end of our junior year."

"And the beginning of our senior year." Then I add, "May it frickin' fly by."

And I watch the girl and the guy. One day, maybe, that would be me and Laila. One day, maybe, not that long from now, that would be me and Laila standing there at the kiosk, hugging a long hello.

At the edge of the commons, a woman strolls by, holding a sheath of papers. She looks familiar, but I can't figure out why. She glances my way and seems to falter.

Dr. Emerson. Is it possible?

I stand up.

Jack asks, "What?'

"I'll be right back." I break into a jog as she rounds the corner of a building, but when I get there, she's gone. Maybe it wasn't her. Maybe she was never there.

As I head back toward Jack, I see a girl in sunglasses about twenty yards away, sitting in the sun, leaning against a tree. I had to have walked right past her, but I was too focused on following the woman. The girl's hair is platinum and long, almost to her waist, and it blows lightly in the breeze. Her blue dress reaches to her ankles, her long legs stretched out in front of her. Her feet are bare. She is reading a book and in one hand, holds a bottle of Yoo-hoo. As I watch, she takes a drink. Frozen, I stand there and watch her drink again.

I pull my phone out of my pocket and stare at it. Maybe this will be the day the call goes through. With a finger, I hit SPEED DIAL. And, like always, I hold my breath and hope.

Faintly, Black Sabbath comes to me on the breeze as the girl reaches beside her and picks up a phone. My phone.

I'm halfway there before she has a chance to answer.

ACKNOWLEDGMENTS

SINCERE THANKS GO OUT TO:

My agent, Scott Mendel, who not only tolerates my crazy story ideas, but somehow manages to find homes for them. A close second is my editor, Liz Szabla, who somehow knows just what questions to ask to bring out the rest of the story. These two are simply the best, and I feel so lucky to have them on my side. And thanks to everyone at Macmillan for their hard work on every aspect of this project.

My early readers, for their support and valuable feedback: Joni, Mark, and the rest of the Puget Sounders, as well as Matt in Paducah, and Brian in Ohio.

Family friend Dr. Kelly Cain, director of the St. Croix Center for Sustainability at my alma mater, UW-River Falls, for letting me pick his brain while writing this novel.

Finally, my husband and daughters, for putting up with my constant angst and obsession (along with the lack of decent meals) when I'm in the middle of a project. I owe you.